# AN ITALIAN DELUSION

Alone in the shadow of the Apennines,
with only a pet rabbit for company,
the exiled hero, when not indulging in erotic fantasies,
harbours thoughts of revenge upon the remote and godlike
eminence who has ousted him from his family business
(at which he was remarkably incompetent)

He is visited by an ex-colleague
whose wife, after a number of mishaps
comic to all but himself
he succeeds in – apparently – seducing.
Triumph brings notions of magnanimity in its wake.
He would nobly destroy the incriminating documents
with which he had planned, in his unregenerate days,
to overthrow his successor. He *would*.
How things turn out quite otherwise,
and the contours of his life reassume their menacing shapes
forms the climax of this sad and often very funny novel,
the self-observed failings and failures of whose hero
many will enjoy recognizing, secretly, as their own.

# An Italian Delusion

OLIVER KNOX

COLLINS
St James's Place, London
1975

William Collins Sons & Co Ltd
London · Glasgow · Sydney · Auckland
Toronto · Johannesburg

First published 1975
© Oliver Knox 1975
ISBN 0 00 221155 6
Set in Monotype Bembo
Made and Printed in Great Britain by
William Collins Sons & Co Ltd Glasgow

*To Richard*

# I

Peter rummaged under the freshly tiled tabletop in the kitchen, and selected one of those polythene bags which Italian shopkeepers used to give liberally to their customers. Out of it he took the beautifully-wrapped slices of salami, the cream cheese, the coffee-beans, the rolls – almost the sum of his day's provisions. Then, with that apologetic air which Englishmen self-consciously affect (one hand to the thinning head) he sidled through a door, and passed two or three workmen rebuilding his chimney. They did not for a second interrupt their labours to glance at him; but he had not felt able to rely on their neglect, and he feared their scorn for the kindly enterprise he was about to undertake.

At the top of the flight of stone steps which led down to the squelchy wasteland of his future garden he stopped, stared at the unseasonably leaden sky and put on his Wellingtons. Clay! Clay! Clay! How he detested it! It sucked at his boots as he walked around hillocks of rubble into one of the stalls which formed the original ground floor of his old farmhouse. Here the builders had stacked a number of discarded beams, charred, wormeaten and spongy, into a higgledy-piggledy lean-to. On other occasions the sight made him groan at the enormity of the building operation he had undertaken, far beyond his resources. Now he simply searched the pile, cooing softly. Nothing. Twice he then skirted the house, peering into the tiny stall where he supposed a pig once to have been kept, turning over a litter of empty cement bags with the toe of a boot, separating the straggly undergrowth of an elder-tree which had somehow survived the builders' devastations. Nothing. At last, when he was clucking his tongue against his palate as the first self-avowal of surrender, his search ended under the ladder, laid sideways outside the old cellar; and he pounced, with commendable agility for a man of middle years whose boots were stuck in the wet clay.

In fact two of the builders' workmen had paused in their cement-mixing, and were observing him. Their eyes continued to follow him as he carried his writhing polythene bag down a steep path bordered by broom, across a pasture rich in herbs, and into a distant patch of scrub oak. By now he was a midget far beneath the house, and the cargo which he squatted to release seemed no larger than a ball of cotton-wool which lopped away, paused and lopped again.

He was well out of earshot. The builders could not hear him call, repeatedly, and softly 'Lops, Lops, Lops!' They would not have been able to comprehend if they had heard. It had been difficult enough – no, impossible – for Peter to explain in the first place, calling some two months ago on the farmer over the hill, that he had wanted to buy a rabbit neither to eat nor to breed but simply to keep as a pet, for company. Indeed, after a few minutes of stammers, of staring at his toes and scratching his head, he had given up the attempt and, foreseeing further complications if he chose the breeding alternative, simply lied that he wanted a rabbit for the table. On the walk home, as it cowered panting against his chest, he had apologized into its ears.

What he was doing now, mercifully he trusted, would certainly cross the borders of Italian understanding. His rabbit might well not survive the marauding huntsmen, the gaitered and solitary men, rifles slung over their shoulders, who prowled and parted the bushes and whistled to their dogs. And there were foxes in the gorge, too. But at least freedom in these thickets, even for a tame rabbit, should have fewer perils than continuing to lop and hop round a home which would be friendless and empty for the next seven days.

However, his rabbit would not leave him, was not tempted by the wilderness. When Peter got up and began his slow ascent it followed him almost like a dog. Only 'almost' because it persisted in circling him anti-clockwise, never allowing itself to be touched, yet keeping close enough for Peter to halt occasionally for fear of stumbling over it. Then he would regain his breath for the next step uphill, while the rabbit sat up and cocked its ears and twitched its front paws, seeming to wait for him. In make-believe Peter put this declining of the gift of freedom down to a returning of his own affection, then (a little closer to reality) to cupboard-love for all the lettuce leaves, the herbs and the not-so-stale chocolate biscuits he had left out for it, after preparing his own lonely supper.

Peter decided to postpone the consideration of the problem by making a detour. There was a rivulet, now in flood from the recent storms, in the gulley which divided his few hectares from his neighbours. He reckoned that if the rabbit could be distracted — for example he might clap his hands in simulation of a gunshot — it might flee, while he forded the stream and hid his scent. In any case he doubted it would be able to swim or jump across.

The manœuvre appeared to succeed. Ten minutes later he reached the high ledge on which his house crouched against a backdrop of bare rock. He had remembered to pocket the empty polythene bag, and with the evidence of his shame concealed was resolute enough to address the workmen.

'You're sure the chimney won't smoke now?'

'It depends. We'll see.'

'Perhaps if one had a top that moved with the wind . . . ?' 'Cowl' was beyond his vocabulary.

'That won't do here. We think we might brick it in so

'... and so ... and so. We must ask Sforza.' Sforza was the builder.

Not for the first time he was forced to admit to himself that he had scarcely any control over the operation, neither over expenditure nor even the design. Of course, this was partly due to his ignorance of building customs in general, and Italian ones in particular. But he doubted whether this was enough to account for his sense of being so completely in the builders' hands. On the few occasions he had believed himself to have reached a clear understanding on some specific matter, and had gone for a day's excursion, he had returned to discover his requests flouted. 'Brown shutters are better. They need less maintenance.' Sometimes he felt as though they were building not a house but a cage for him, and that he was thus now doubly or trebly a prisoner. But remonstration had always been disagreeable to him, and surrender came easily after a few philosophical reflections.

He retreated, climbing to the single, top-storey room which in self-mocking *folie de grandeur* he had named 'The Tower Room'. This did, indeed, form a small turret, whose front wall gave an effect of leaning backwards so that, seen from the valley with half-closed eyes, there could be conjured up a resemblance to the tower of a Himalayan monastery. In this room he intended soon – Ah, all his good intentions! – to begin his studies of the poets of the Duecento. Amateur studies only, he would deprecatingly confess. But they would, or so he thought, give him some identification with the new landscape of his life, they would soften his exile, they would dim the injustice he fancied to have been inflicted on himself.

His few belongings were still scattered, mostly on the floor, awaiting the accommodation of promised shelves. From one corner he picked up a pair of binoculars. With his knees splayed, in a position like that which gym instructors made him adopt long ago in morning prep-school exercises (*one-two-three-four*), he squatted to look out of the window—low as it was, and shielded with heavy eaves from the threat of the sun.

With motionless wings, a hawk circled over the gulley from which he had just clambered. Some white specks turned out to be boulders. A red Fiat scuttled on a distant ridge. Of Lops there was no sign.

# 2

The two builders, over their picnic wine and spaghetti, discussed him briefly. They could not fathom what madness drove this sad and sallow Englishman to live alone in a peasant's house in the Marches of Italy. Although they had worked as mates for weeks they still did not talk freely to each other.

'It could be political, but I think not.'
'Some woman, perhaps.'
'What was he doing with that rabbit?'
'He has lots of money, look at his car, the crafty ones are robbing him.'
'It's none of our affair.'
'He should fence his land from huntsmen.'
'They were out searching for snails last night.'
'If they catch his rabbit, it's his fault.'
'Why doesn't he live in the city?'

And so on. No wonder the builders were at a loss. Peter was unable to explain to himself why he was where he was, or to admit the causes of his downfall and expulsion. He preferred to take refuge in bravado, though you would not have guessed it from his timid manner. Only in the bleakness of the small hours did he lick his wounded vanity, before indulging in erotic fantasies, at which he was rather good.

Now he began to prepare for tomorrow's early departure for Venice – selecting a tie from this piece of floor and socks from that with maundering finickitiness. Although two months' solitude had scarcely softened his rancour, he was looking forward with wan amusement to the meeting with his former chief colleague and enemy. He called to mind as he scraped clay from his only good pair of shoes, the dome of the man's forehead, the whinny of his laugh, the overbearing joviality which served to conceal his lack of friendliness and (he was obliged to admit) the force of his intellect. Peter had never decided what part J.D. had played in the swoop of the final intrigue.

He remembered their conversation after the last supper. J.D. had grown even more affable towards the end.

'Well, I can't tell you how much we shall all miss you here. Your contribution . . .'

'I shan't expect to be recalled from exile.'

'Ha. Ha. Ha. Ha. Especially your *particular* friends you've done so much for.'

'Well, I hope you continue to make money.'

'If only for our pensioners' sake! There will be a number of loose ends. A weekend in Venice would not be disagreeable. I shall visit you.' He consulted a large well-kept diary.

Perhaps in retrospect, the conversation hadn't been good-natured at all.

After his desultory preparations Peter devoted very little more thought to the dismissal of Lops, although – more through habit than sentiment – when he took his evening stroll after the builders had gone, he did peer into one or two of its former resting-places.

It was while Peter was inspecting the wild thyme (which he had plundered from the meadow below, to plant in a walled bed he had himself built around a fig-tree) that he became aware of the approach of visitors. Laughter was coming round the corner of the drive. The fresh-laid gravel had given visitors the courage to approach his refuge on foot.

He wondered whether to hide, and had indeed turned towards one of the stalls to do so, but irresolution betrayed him. A glance over his shoulder had convinced him his guests were now so close that they must already have sighted him.

There was nothing to do but to pull up his trousers – Peter had grown thin in Italy – pat down his hair, fumble for his spectacles, and turn to face his intruders. They continued to laugh and scrunch up the gravel noisily, coming at him three abreast.

Peter's eyes were caught by a flutter of colours – chiefly the red, blue and white of three bulky umbrellas, folded floppily, carried high so that not even their thick wooden ferrules would be smeared by clay. Scarlet galoshes clashed with mauve tights. Conical black mackintosh hats hid most of the faces. Peter now had realized by whom, sweetly and unexpectedly, he was being visited. It was his student, whose beauty had been slyly extolled by the acquaintance who had introduced her. She was accompanied by two of her girl-friends: for the sake of propriety, Peter assumed.

The idea had been that the student and he should instruct each other in the use of their native tongues. Before the first meeting Peter had given rein to delectable visions about the possibilities of lessons with her: the idioms of courtesy leading to those of intimacy, innocent games of 'I Spy' to less innocent ones . . . The mutual acquaintance had gone so far as to hint with a smirk at voluptuosity, *sensualità*, and although Peter reminded himself that a young student was unlikely to possess Titianesque charms, this had not stopped him imagining the curve of her thighs as she lay, fingering a dictionary. Alas for reality! She was a slim and shrill girl whose few faint intimations of sex were conveyed by her eyes – wide, soft, doe eyes very heavily made up with jet black eyelashes. And even those, Peter soon realized, sent no invitation but merely conformed to fashion – proving that their owner was a sophisticated child of the city.

It was brave of her to call upon him. Up until now they had had about half a dozen assignations in different bars in the city centre. He would press a drink upon her, she would decline but accept a sticky cake, he would experiment at random with the multitudinous garish liqueurs – sniffing doubtfully and sipping courageously. Then they would try to make themselves heard over the background of jukebox, billiard table and the odd flare-ups of argumentative wrath at nearby tables. As a language course it had limitations. Conversation had not advanced beyond the discovery of passport facts about themselves and their families, the number of brothers and sisters, the survival or death of parents, occupations, abodes.

Peter envied the seeming copybook simplicity of her background. Her sketches of it were so straightforward. But *he* had no brother who was a car mechanic in Ancona with three children (two boys, one girl). *He* had no father who was a wine and oil merchant in the Marches. It was beyond him, so he thought, to convey what it was like to have been a tycoon in the Midlands as his loved and long-dead father had been, or to paint the life of a single child brought up in that sombre and austere mansion on the outskirts of a wealthy suburb. He had no close relations surviving. He did allow himself to hint at his previous wealth and position, but omitted to confess to her its nepotic origins. Nor did he lecture her on the liberal and democratic principles he had unwisely endeavoured to introduce into his business. These, he felt, would not translate easily into Italian. And he wished to refer to his wife, separated from him for so many years, in no more than a single sentence.

'We felt sorry for you, we thought you might be spending the holiday all alone and you would like visitors' said his student in a rush, fluttering her eyelashes and advancing to within a centimetre of him. She continued to urge herself against his body as he backed awkwardly towards the wall of the well-house. Peter had discovered to his sorrow that it was not sexual search but only extreme short sight which led to these groping assaults. The others giggled.

'Wouldn't you like to see inside, come in please,' stuttered Peter, glancing nervously up and away at the clouds, and biting one of the arms of his spectacles. 'Please, your boots, don't worry, everything's in a mess, I'm afraid.'

They were shaking themselves like wet dogs. One of them twisted her neck to look up the half-restored chimney. Another with a tiny squeal kicked off a boot halfway across the floor. Numbers made them bold. As Peter made fresh coffee – they deserved better than the reheated jug he had proposed to allow himself – he decided he was touched by their chirruping solicitude. He sat down in his rocking chair to face them, and hoped that he did not look too schoolmasterish.

'My builders were working today. Actually, I'd forgotten it was a holiday.'

'And for Easter? You're going back to England for Easter?'

'I can't.'

There was a long pause. He had an impulse to explain why he couldn't return. In his own tongue, or to English girls of such slight acquaintance, this would have embarrassed him dreadfully. But he felt a foreign language gave him cover. And the plea of ignorance would allow him to falter or to stop if the going became too painful.

# 3

'I'm a sort of exile,' began Peter. 'It's a long story.'

'An exile! Like Napoleon in Elba!'

'We're going to Elba this summer. Relatives have a house by the sea.'

'It's very beautiful, Elba.'

Peter smiled, and cleared his throat. He was piqued by losing his audience. 'Perhaps I'm being too romantic,' he said. It occurred to him that the old schoolboy phrase 'sent to Coventry' in some ways described his case more accurately. He wondered where Coventry was in Italy. 'Real exiles are sent to Siberia nowadays, aren't they? I can hardly call this Siberia. No – I can't, I don't complain of physical hardship, except for all this wet and clay.' In company, his self-pity evaporated. Alone, he would reflect that one can eat one's heart out as painfully in Italy as in any other region of the world.

'Surely you get mud in England, too,' said one of the girls, prettier than the others. She twiddled her bare toes, looking at them absently. Peter doubted whether he was making any progress. Their sympathy did not, indeed, depend on any knowledge of the details of his case. Nor did he mind remaining an enigma. But he would like to convey a faint halo of nobility, or at least of importance, if that could be managed without obvious boasting. Yet, when it came down to it, whatever had he really contributed to the success of the business that bore his name? When he was younger, before his recurrent attacks of migraine, he had certainly been a remarkable diagnostician, a forecaster of the future – a sort of marketing seer; but his analytic and prognostic gifts were more of backroom than of boardroom calibre; and it was very doubtful whether he would ever have climbed so high, or been tolerated so long, had he not been his father's son.

'I managed to put my family firm – a large one, several thousand employees – almost entirely in the hands of the workers. It was an experiment in industrial management. You read about "worker power" in Italy, don't you?'

'They're young extremists. Some of them criminals. They throw bombs.'

'Quite a lot was written about my plan,' went on Peter doggedly. 'Left-wing members of Parliament, like your senators, visited my – the workers' – factories.'

The time had not come for him to admit that the experiment had ended in disaster and that sound, hard-faced men had eventually ousted him with contempt, and taken successful control.

'It was featured on television, too.' He remembered his appearances well. Now he recalled, inconsequentially, the make-up studio where he had been led before the programme; and how he had yielded, bewildered, to the care of the cosmeticians who had wished to 'improve' his sallow countenance.

'You don't have a television here, do you,' said one of the girls. 'You don't look after yourself. You need us to look after you.'

Another said, 'You tell us all you did for your workers. What good have they done for you?'

Yes, Peter thought, he *had* devoted most of the first fifty-three years of his life to attempting to benefit others. Perhaps it was true that he had paid insufficient attention – that was the dry phrase his ex-colleagues used – to the motives of profit, too much to the interests of his workers and to the quality of his products.

'What did your factory make?' asked the girl who was not only prettier but also more inquisitive than the others. Peter decided against a dissertation on the trials and rewards of large-scale confectionery manufacture. Unlikely that he would hold the attention of his audience by explaining to them the differences between, say, the many kinds of chocolate flake on the market (at one time his firm alone had produced a dozen such 'lines'). In any case, the talk would have been both tantalizing and churlish without the proffering of samples, an adequate supply of which he had neglected to bring into exile. In the old days, the ritual of 'tasting' lines, the solemn munching of samples marshalled down the centre of the boardroom table, had always accompanied discussion of costs, of graphs of market trends, of distribution and so forth.

Peter gave his rocking-chair one or two gentle shoves. Then he wiped his spectacles carefully and holding them near their frame between finger and thumb, pointed them towards the settee. He assumed an air of tired and pale benignity. His former colleagues would have recognized and been duly maddened by this familiar stalling technique. They would have known that, in the manner of a shifty politician, he was about to answer an earlier (or even completely different) question, not the one he had been asked.

'Don't Italian parents teach you never to expect gratitude? I don't know, perhaps that's an English attitude. But anyway I didn't succeed, you know, in giving all my – the – workers the freedom I should have liked. It's very difficult to put into practice.'

They stared at him uncomprehendingly. He remembered the scroll illuminated in blue and gold, with which he had once been presented by the workers to commemorate his family's building of the firm, and which used to hang in the boardroom. He remembered it with a prick of shame, for he had not always stood aloof from his colleagues' mockery of it. He remembered, too, the gift of a day's work on the occasion of some national emergency. This formed the sum of the 'gratitude' he had received from the workers.

On the other hand, as he could have reminded himself, the financial control of the firm had always been left ingeniously beyond the workers' grasp; and only two years ago, he had presided over abortive negotiations to merge with a foreign competitor whose business 'ethics' were quite other than his own.

Peter began to doubt whether it would divert the girls to be told how or why he had been driven into exile. In fact, certain knowledge he possessed made it so desirable in some people's eyes he should reside abroad, that his principal colleague had not been content to urge upon him the fiscal advantages of emigration – but had gone so far as to insist upon his physical removal from England, as a condition of a generous pension. There was no point in even hinting at all this. It did not put him in a very favourable light.

'Don't think I'm like Achilles sulking in his tent. I really am an exile, but I can travel all over the world so long as I never set foot in my own country again. I'm off to Venice for three days now. This summer I shall go to Greece. Egypt, possibly this winter. Most people would envy me.'

He got up and brought down from a shelf a beautiful brass Aladdin lamp, removed its hood with care and lit it. He loved the softness of its light. But the girls seemed flabbergasted.

'Surely they'll give you light. They must bring electricity soon,' said one.

'I don't know. It doesn't matter. I rather like this.'

'He prefers to live like a peasant,' said the pretty girl to her neighbour. 'I've heard of other cases.'

'We must get home before it's dark,' they chorused. 'We left our car at the bottom of the hill. Your drive is so rocky.'

'I can't just let you leave like this,' said Peter. 'You've had nothing, not even a drink.' Then there was some giggling and nudging and quick Italian talk which Peter was unable to follow. The boldest of the three said: 'Do you think we could ask you to lend us some English books? Something light? Not Shakespeare. I think Shakespeare would be too difficult. Something modern. Perhaps a book of a film we have all seen.'

They began to list recent films. A slight frown clouded one girl's brow. 'On the whole,' she said in the most matter-of-fact tone, '*not* pornography. I don't understand very well *il pornografico nuovo*. Do you like it?' She spoke as if it were a reputable new art form, though one which for better or worse her own cultural antennae did not allow her to appreciate.

'More, perhaps, of a masculine taste,' agreed Peter in an equally serious voice.

'That is what I have heard friends say. Possibly it is only a fashion. If it is, I do not think we have to study it.'

Peter got up and noticed, across the general disarray, one of the cardboard packing-cases in a corner full of books. A cover of an old, seldom-consulted English dictionary hung limply down the side of the carton, like a dog's ear. He walked to the other side of the room and glanced at the titles of the books – a few contemporary novels for railway-train reading, nothing too exacting, nothing eligible to be classed as pornography. He lugged the whole carton back to the girls with a show of robustness. 'Take them all,' he said. 'Take the box. I'm afraid the dictionary is a bit battered. Like me,' he added, deprecatingly.

Peter had begun to be accustomed to the all-or-nothing quality of living in Italy – days of Arcadian calm (which, however, left him uneasy) followed by days of violent irruptions; catastrophes like thunderbolts, unheralded happenings like gusts of storms. Today certainly seemed a day of action. As he opened the door for his parting guests, their chorus of *'ciaos'* was shattered by the crackle and crescendo staccato of some beastly machine. Noise seemed to squib all over the place, echoing from rock to rock. It preceded, Peter saw, a black figure sliding and banging down his drive on a motor-bicycle. The man descended only a foot from the porch. His boots seemed to glisten, even in the dusk. He parted the girls with one sweep of his arm, and put a foot on the second step of the stairs, looking up at Peter with the arrogance of uniformed youth.

'You are Peter,' he said, more as a statement than an interrogative. Peter blinked and nodded. The man said 'sign' and extracted four pieces of paper from his black case. Peter backed into the house, towards the Aladdin. Two of the pieces of paper were telegrams, two receipts.

'Venice postponed sorry J.D.' said one. No explanation. The second was in the more discursive style of another old colleague. 'Shall be in your neck of the woods on our Italian tour Thursday hope Helen and I see you Oliver.' Were the two telegrams sent in collusion? Their date-stamps were the same. Peter decided to postpone speculation on the point.

The splay-armed figure was already crouched like Batman on his machine. He revved it, tyres tore into the wet gravel and the girls were spattered. Peter felt he might have gone to their aid; instead he shut the door and re-read the telegram, attempting to extract hidden meanings, find clues to conspiracies. He had always imagined the most apparently innocuous of telegrams conveyed menace; and the arrival of two simultaneously, in the sudden Italian dusk, made him very uneasy indeed, made him feel as though he were some puppet – some articulated, elderly doll jerked in spasms by figures usually invisible, who might yet appear at their whim through the parting of thunderclouds. Neither telegram called for any reply, so he was not left even with the comfort of devising counter-action.

He shivered a little as he adjusted the settee. It was a pity he could not yet light the fire – wooden props were still supporting an arch. He felt too chill and too unhinged to derive solace from the poets of the Duecento. He decided to nibble at some salami, drink a whole litre of wine, let fantasies grow in his mind like balloons, and exclude self-pity (or indeed self-enquiry of any sort).

'Oliver is a weak fool, but I would not mind his wife,' he thought brutally, the wine instilling sexually aggressive thoughts quite incongruous to his appearance, which remained benign and gently apologetic. Indeed became more so, due to dishevelment. Helen! He thought for a while of her grey eyes, her air of indolent sensuality just the tempting side of blowsiness, her cosseted fullness which suited so well the expensive cars in which she was accustomed to travel. He pictured her mouth sucking at a large ice-cream.

The west wind made a join of his kerosene-stove chimney whine and squeak, until the noise drilled his ears and diverted him from pursuit of his imaginary lusts. Given such feebleness, would he be up to the seduction of Oliver's wife? The surroundings certainly did not help. Perhaps if the hot weather came? True, there was a sheepskin rug on the bed, but Helen was used to more opulent comforts than those he could now provide. And that fond and languorous look she had once bestowed on him – was he sure it was really intended for his eyes only, not casually sent out to the world at large? How would he be able to persuade Oliver to absent himself for long enough? He might perhaps direct him to the deep and wooded ravine where the wild asparagus grew, and encourage him to gather it. What stupidity! Anyway, Oliver was far too lazy. Thinking of the ravine, he was reminded of Lops. His dismissal had been proved premature, he need not have consigned him so soon to the freedom of the wilderness.

The litre bottle almost empty, he reaffirmed to himself

his earlier vow to exclude self-pity from his evening circum-meditations. Who, he nevertheless demanded, had suffered more than he had from betrayal or treachery? Who could have?

# 4

Peter awoke the next morning to realize he had a spare few days when his calendar told him he ought to be in Venice. He had discovered that although there was no certain rescue from the waves of loneliness which at times all but submerged him, one means of keeping his head above water was to construct routines – hourly, daily, weekly, monthly, ones. 9–10 improve Italian, 10–11 speak builders, 11–11.30 wax tiled floor. And so on. He would come across snippets of such discarded routines in odd corners (behind a chest, say, or stuck on the end of a builder's drill) and squint at them to remember if he had duly performed his tasks.

These minor servitudes occupied what would otherwise have been the intolerable vacuum of absolute freedom.

Peter then determined on these two dangerously 'free' days to make an excursion. He would walk in the high Apennines, whose ridges (like the teeth of a giant's upturned saw) dentellated his western horizon.

He had read in the Victorian Baedeker, which was one of the few possessions he had taken from home, of a monastery which lay at the upper end of a wooded valley. He was intrigued by the gloomy descriptions, and hoped that it still lay beyond the ordinary run of charabancs. In any case he intended to descend on it from one of the mule-tracks which climbed and dipped along the crests of the mountains.

He boiled his egg and started to study his maps. No

clatter of builders interrupted his gently wheezing concentration. It was Saturday. Surely no one would come to his house today – not even the postwoman (the stones of his drive, she had informed him, were too sharp, she would deliver his mail in future only as far as the village below).

The stillness of his isolation was given intensity by the mist, enveloping even the fig-tree a few yards from his window. Hardly the weather, he thought, pouting out his lower lip, for the walk which he had imposed on himself. He would not be deterred. He would, however, select with extra foresight the paraphernalia he might need.

Perhaps it was the mist which changed his customary sense of perspective. Every object he took up, he gazed at close to, as though through a magnifying-glass. He held a walking-boot right up to his face, examining each nail, scraping off each particle of caked clay. He opened and shut his knife half-a-dozen times and wiped it to peer at the minute legend on the base of the large blade. Deciding to change his socks, he cut his toe-nails, and crinkled his nose as he held up the yellowed cut slices and sniffed them.

Such meticulous practices were not a means of postponing his departure. Nor were they solely due to his plethora of spare time. They were rather a hugging of the space and of the objects immediately around, to lend him comfort from the greyness which enclosed him – as though the mist was encircling with the slow swirls of its cloak even the man who sat, hunched, inside his house on the ledge.

But there are some gaols whose bars can be broken by acts of will, and Peter was only one hour late in setting off. A further hour was wasted in a gorge where builders were dynamiting.

'You can't pass. You should have seen the signs', one of them shouted above his many-toothed earthshifter.

Peter waved his arms. 'There were no signs.' A boulder tumbled slowly down the cliff.

'Wait. Patience.'

Peter descended to the green Apennine stream, and laid his compass this way and that on the map. This further delay threw in doubt his arrival at the monastery by nightfall. But at least the mist was clearing. By two o'clock, he had arrived just beneath the mountain-pass traversed by the road. Two or three wooden chairs, battered and forlorn, stood on a terrace outside a café whose windows were still shuttered. He was reminded of damp Cotswold walks in his youth, so much so that he asked for a cup of tea – before arranging to leave his car and discussing his route.

'There is only one path to the monastery. But your car has done most of the climbing.'

'Yes. I follow the rim. How long . . . ?'

'Four hours if you walk fast. When you get to the monastery, ring the bell outside the gate. They will answer however late. Only one thing – there is a parting of three ways. Don't take either the right or the left, which lead down into other villages, but continue straight.'

Peter marched briskly along a forest bridleway soft with leafmould – well-kept and regularly drained with wooden conduits. Columns and columns of beeches surrounded him. It was hard to tell whether the light-green shimmer in the middle distance came from tree-trunks or from emergent leaves. Occasionally rocks two or three times his height overhung his way, giving into dark, red-mouthed caverns fit for troglodytes. The going was easy. He met no one.

A precipice, marked by a white wound in the mountain face, struck up at him, and he lifted his feet carefully over the stump of a tree and blinked twice to banish vertigo. A hawk hovered beneath him.

After an hour a hummock emerged from the dusk. It reminded Peter of a wart on the ridge of a nose. Until now the path had led him unmistakably along the edge of an escarpment. Now one footpath straggled up to the top of the dome (or wart), another plunged to the right, and a third continued boldly as before – but veering downhill to the left. Peter decided that he had probably arrived at the parting of the ways spoken of by the forester. Not wishing to descend, he left the bridleway and climbed the middle footpath up towards the top of the dome. The phalanxes of beech were left behind and beneath. The path trickled and twisted and branched between thickets – of hazel, Peter thought, but it was growing too dark to be sure.

Unseen brambles tugged and tore at his ankles. Swerving wings shadowed him and made him involuntarily cower – an owl, probably, for screeches and echoes of screeches began to come at him. Higher, lower, farther, nearer. This was all very well, but whatever had happened to the path? Peter felt ridiculously indignant at this encirclement by the forces of nature. Crouching down, he attempted to study his damp map. A few very distant lights, sprinkled near the heads of valleys, gave him no clue. There was nothing for it but to proceed westward, across a series of gulleys which looked like black slits, in the hope of finding another (or, even better, his original) track. The relief he felt when this reassuring evidence of man's work gleamed white at him! It was, it must be, *his* path leading with Roman straightness to the top of another small peak. Yes – and there in front was the true and easily decipherable 'parting of the ways'. Peter scrambled down the bank and did not even wince at twisting his ankle. He hobbled on his way.

A moon began to make its seductive suggestions – for example, leading Peter to see, in his hope that he was nearing the monastery, a tall cross by the margins of his bridleway. (In fact, it proved to be a fir with broken branches and a forked top.) Next, an Alpine tinkle of bells delighted him, and he saw he was walking across a pasture populated with white oxen. Surely this must be a monastery herd. He began to look confidently for a track off the ridge, down to his destination.

A blanket of mist idly and insinuatingly began to form around his feet. It gave him the illusion that the lower half of his legs no longer belonged to him – and also, he realized, it must obscure the turning-off he sought. He groped between two bushes which *could* have been sentinels guarding a path; but a brief clamber and a glimpse of a precipice soon made him gasp uphill again to the ridgeway. He could see from his compass, and from the pole-star, too, that the track which half an hour earlier had seemed so friendly and certain, was now leading him far too far to the south. He sheltered under a bush, shivered from the night air, sucked at his last chocolate bar, and again consulted his map. 'A fix, I am in a fix' he repeated to himself out loud, wondering for the first time what to do if he failed to reach the monastery that night.

He determined to retrace his steps towards the ox herd, reckoning that there must be some track near their pasture. Or, at the worst, he would take refuge in a shed: there must, *must*, be a shed. Then, at his most gloomy moment, he suddenly sighted the lights of the monastery clustered below him – five hundred feet or so down. All should now be plain sailing. In his relief he flashed the beam of his torch everywhere along the border of the path, *willing* it, without success, to pierce the mist.

But by the time he had again reached the pasture of white oxen – who were half-floating like himself in the layer of cloud – his anxiety had returned.

The torch was dimming, the path still unfound. The oxen were now immobile, probably sleeping, and he could hear their heavy breathing. Somehow their stillness and shapes (torsos of statues truncated by the mist) seemed to be menacing. He cleared his throat, and called 'MOO' appeasingly to them, and felt foolish. He circled their pasture, knee deep in wet grass and fringed by inhospitable scrub. Suddenly the lights of the monastery, which had twinkled and beckoned him down through the forest below, were extinguished. It must be later than he thought. Damn – his watch had stopped. Clearly he was being beset by a swarm of pretty vexations, typical of his new life in this foreign land.

He cursed himself for having failed to take a bearing on the monastery lights. 'I've spent lots of my life interfering with other people's lives, I seem very bad at planning my own,' he muttered through his teeth.

He trod on something soft and squelchy – surely it was too early in the year, and too high and too cold, for snakes to be out? All the same, he shuddered, and wiped cold sweat away with his sleeve. Exhaustion was making him foolish.

A dark shape like a wigwam loomed ahead of him. It proved to be a crude palisade, protecting a cone of sodden hay. Peter decided to burrow into it and take a fitful rest – perhaps even to doze, but it was compressed very densely and sliced like cheese, and it took Peter a bad half hour before he had scratched out enough to make a tolerable nest. However, now he was at least warm – even if damp, prickled and fearful of the surrounding nightlife. He ground his teeth with irritation at his failure. He wondered whether there was some flaw in his character which led to his so seldom reaching his goal. He felt safe in examining his character with only the oxen for company – as though at other times, even in his remote farmhouse, he feared that self-examination might travel on waves of air and be overheard. He extracted a stalk from his ear. Did he cheat, perhaps? Ah, there was a word. But only from the best motives! Except perhaps when he was a schoolboy.

He remembered furtive cribbing, and his early mastery of the art of upside-down-reading. Character – what was *character* anyway? Memories of his itchy and inky prep-school days led him to a tall, sneering assistant master called Hadley. Hadley was double-jointed and enjoyed playing with his finger and thumb. He had once caught Peter by the scruff of his neck, let him go, caught him again and tweaked his ears.

'Let me go, sir, please let me go.'
'Tell me why I should.'
'I'm not doing anything wrong.'
'How do I know?'
'I'm not a bad character, sir.'
'Bad character? The trouble with you isn't that you have a bad character – it's just that you haven't got any character at all.'

Yet (perhaps through cunning) Peter had not done too badly, after all was said and done. Business circles had at times regarded him as a moderate success, his colleagues had afforded him occasional respect, his friends had given him qualified affection, his wife had tolerated him for ages, and a few whose wells of love were fed by generous springs of pity had even – yes – loved him. True, his 'idealism' had got him nowhere, could even be said to have destroyed him, reduced him to this shivering creature huddled beneath a few straws. Even this predicament, he reminded himself, was not a genuine one, it was of his own contriving and inept execution, and it was very temporary (unless he caught pneumonia).

At the first insipid suggestion of dawn, Peter decided to abandon efforts to sleep, and to walk on. Quite soon he found a brambly path leading downhill onto a spur from which he could make out the roofs of the monastery plainly, still very far below. He was cheered by a few rays of sun. Seeing a tall Baptist-like figure in the distance, he attempted to repair the worst of his disarray.

A mountain shepherd and his sheep came nearer. Peter would probably have avoided him – his love for his fellow-men being at the low ebb which dawn commonly brings – but for his need to learn the way.

'You need to rejoin the ridge and follow it for an hour.'
'But last night I searched everywhere . . .'
'The path to the monastery leads downhill on the other side of the mountain.'

Peter didn't see how it could. Perhaps he had misunderstood. 'The mist . . .'

'Ah! You must have had a wretched night in the open. Take this, it is all I have. We are poor people.' He gave Peter a slice of sheep's cheese. Two military aircraft wheeled and whined ferociously above them, drowning Peter's thanks.

'If only they could spend more money on us, and less on wars. I had seven years of war. Albania, Africa. War is mad.'

Peter wasn't inclined to enter on the rationale of defence expenditure. Italian for 'The price of freedom is eternal vigilance' would have had an excellent ring, but it seemed inapposite to the time and place. However, some response was called for. Evidently the man wanted a political discussion. Perhaps it was to compensate for a solitary way of life. A bromide would be best.

'To have one's own country fought over, too. That's even more terrible. Difficult for an Englishman like myself to understand.'

'If there were a God how would he allow such things?' continued the shepherd, in sorrow. 'How could he, tell me that?'

Peter thought that an unfair price was being extracted for his cheese.

'Isn't it true man is free to . . .' he stuttered, about to deploy one of the standard justifications for the existence of a deity.

'Free!' interrupted the shepherd derisorily. 'Aren't we all slaves? Poverty makes us slaves.'

'I admit that I am one of the fortunate people. I've not been really poor,' confessed Peter. He easily forgave himself the mendacity of his 'really'. But it was ridiculous, he thought afterwards, to have been so defensive – to have indulged in those feelings of guilt so common among second-generation capitalists of the educated middle-class.

'People who have never been slaves don't know,' said the shepherd.

Peter doubted very much whether this was true. Or, rather, he supposed everyone at some time or another must have felt himself ensnared in the toils of necessity. Certainly there were occasions when he desired – wistfully and fancifully – to emulate those fairground exhibitionists who writhe, kneeling on the ground, and escape from their fetters with pretended agonizing and actual ease. But he preferred to shirk argument about the awareness of slaves.

His immediate concern after all was entirely practical – to cut short this encounter, to return to his car and his home, to wash and eat and drink; and to prepare for the arrival of Oliver and his wife. Discussion with this gaunt and unwontedly truculent shepherd was not going to help him. He managed without difficulty to divert the conversation to an elucidation of the best route, and to turn and hold up his hand in farewell, after gulping the remainder of the dry cheese. As he walked away, he hoped he had not disgraced himself. He was sad, though, to have abandoned the visit to the monastery. It was another small failure.

# 5

In Peter's earlier life the dread of taking almost any decision – particularly in the company of others – had often brought him attacks of migraine. There were times when he could justly be accused of being in a panic of irresolution. Such habits, perhaps even more than the vaunted principles he would attempt to bring to bear on simple day-to-day affairs, had exasperated his colleagues. Now that he had been forcibly retired, he had managed, if not to eliminate the necessity of taking any decisions, at least to narrow the areas of choice to less taxing questions such as, say, the type of salami or the colour of eggs to buy.

At first this holiday – for such it almost seemed – had come as a relief and his migraines ceased. But gradually he became aware of a sinister reversal of roles between himself and the world. Instead of his acting, however irresolutely, upon his surroundings he began to feel acted upon. Builders, shopkeepers, motor-cars, even trees and stones seemed to shed their obedience or passivity and turn on him. It was a long list of hostile activity.

Poetry was some escape from persecution. He thought of melancholy Jacques. Perhaps his symptoms were the usual ones among new recluses. And perhaps the reappearance of familiar faces and the sound of English accents would mitigate, even eliminate them. Solitude impairs, and the resumption of social activity might restore some equilibrium to the active/passive, hunter/hunted scales in which we are all placed (or place ourselves). Those scales were 'real' enough to Peter at least in the sense that he felt himself weighed in them, quite as vividly as he experienced any other perception whatsoever.

On a fine evening two days later Oliver did indeed bluster in with the insensitive bonhomie which Peter so well remembered (and which Helen, trailing around after him, appeared to tolerate with vague affection). Oliver stood with his back to the cliff-face, gazed over the folds of mountains, and jingled coins in his pocket.

'You're well out of it, old boy. Well out of it. You left at the right time. You old devil. Capital view you've got.'

Helen said, 'It's very romantic of you, I think. Being so far away. But you always were a bit of a romantic, weren't you? Behind those spectacles.' Peter was delighted.

'That's a fair-sized old mountain you've got over there,' went on Oliver. 'How high? Any idea?'

'Well, it's not exactly mine,' said Peter.

Helen said, 'Wild flowers, isn't it? You always loved them. It must be a wonderful place for wild flowers.' Peter was deflated. He had never collected wild flowers in his life. He knew nothing about them.

Oliver blundered on. 'How long will it take us to do this bit of Italy, would you say? See all there is to see, I mean? You first, of course. You're the sight we've really come to see.'

Peter fixed his eyes on a giant snail, and the silvery slither it had left on a boulder. When they were picked up those snails would retreat slothfully into their shells – the unpursuable withdrawal of a creature scarcely outgoing in the first place. Oliver's joviality gave Peter a feeling of kinship with the snail. He didn't reply.

'We've brought the usual messages. I'm not sure you will – some will make you smile, bring back the old days.'

Peter had never been clear whose 'side' Oliver was on.

Did it matter? Did he care any longer? He brought himself to ask: 'And how is J.D. doing?'

'Firmly in the saddle. Changing a lot. Hardly recognize the old place. Yes, J.D. has certainly got the bit between his teeth. You'd be surprised.'

Peter almost missed the metaphorical muddle – was J.D. the rider or the horse? – in tune as it was with his own disequilibrium. Perhaps a drink or two might help to divert talk away from the raking-over of old days, or news of present ones. He would like to be able to say that both topics bored him. In fact, they clouded his eyes with apprehension and made his bowels faintly queasy.

Soon Oliver had helped himself to a second large whisky from the bottle which he had kindly presented to Peter. He was showing no awareness that Peter found the direction of his talk in any way discomfiting. Meanwhile, Helen had sauntered a little way down the path and was kneeling, probably to examine some herb, and shaking back her long blonde hair. Peter's eyes and some of his thoughts followed her. She was too good for Oliver. Her features weren't fine, they were too round and soft for that. Her indolent and fond air reminded Peter of one of the white oxen with whom he had exchanged stares on his mountain walk. But Helen was sensual, too. Languor in a woman appealed to him.

Peter was continuing to pretend to Oliver that he was listening half-heartedly, and to pretend to himself that he wasn't listening at all. In fact his contemplation of Helen still allowed him to pay adequate attention to Oliver, who could be relied upon to repeat himself.

'Your mistake was to trust people you had helped. Stupid, that,' Oliver was saying.

'I'd forgotten how much I had appreciated Scotch,' said Peter.

'Still, you know, if you wanted . . . Don't think you ought to moulder here forever. Don't think you need to.'

'I think I shall be able to give my solitary life some aim. I certainly hope so.'

'Come on, come on, who was it who said, "You're never *well* out of it. Just *out* of it?" Can't remember. Seriously, though. You've still got cards to play. You know you have.'

'And you're saying all this off your own bat?'

'Perhaps you're right,' said Oliver without answering Peter's last question. 'Perhaps the time isn't ripe for a comeback. But you keep in touch, don't you? You should.'

'No. I don't. At all,' said Peter. Then he thought that was too curt an answer to Oliver's seemingly well-meant bumbles. After all, it was just possible to take Oliver at his face value, so why not do so? Even if there were hidden meanings, he no longer had great interest in unravelling them. So he added, 'I'm really and truthfully putting down roots here for good. It's a slow job, of course.'

Oliver caught sight of Peter's continuing gaze at Helen and clapped him on the back, more affably than ever. He must have detected a snub. Peter savoured a second's remorse. The bluff are not always insensitive, he thought.

'Roots or not, old boy, how about joining us on an expedition? Getting out of yourself a bit?'

The word 'expedition' made Peter wince at his recent fiasco. An unconscious retaliation of Oliver's, he thought.

Oliver squinted at the landscape. 'Over the hills and far away. Like the nursery rhyme.'

'Well, I've just come back really. From a monastery you might enjoy visiting. I'll show you on the map after dinner. Explain the way.' Peter half-lied at the time because it was easier.

'Roots you said?' Oliver took up the word again and branched out in a different direction. 'Yes, there's a lot of planting to be done. I can see that. You must pick Helen's brains. She'd like that. She's the gardener. Shouldn't be surprised if you didn't make a splendid affair of it.'

Was there an innuendo? Oliver's tone was surely too jovial to contain subtlety. But he would certainly be glad to accept the loan of Helen, in any capacity. She was at that moment trailing back up the path. Her wispy traces of tiredness – for example, she was carrying the wild flowers she had plucked *upside down* – did not make her any the less attractive.

Oliver raised his voice towards her. 'I was just asking our good friend Peter when he was going to start on his Italian country garden. Singing your praises, and now here you come, pulling his things up.'

'They're wild lupins,' said Helen. 'Very early ones. Later on you can eat the beans. They're good.' She flumped down and laughed for no discernible reason – a low laugh which sounded confiding but whose origin was probably shyness. She laid a finger on her lips, like a child, and for a few seconds none of them spoke.

'I was thinking of animals, too. Have you thought of keeping animals, Peter? You've got enough ground, I imagine. Enough space in the farmhouse, too. Even mangers,' Helen said.

Peter wondered whether to confess about Lops. He was not sure, but he might have caught sight of him that dawn, nibbling a rose. Perhaps . . . but how *could* he have found his way back? Though the story might amuse Helen vaguely, Oliver would be certain to mock him.

'The trouble is animals make one a prisoner,' began Peter.

'So do gardens, if you look after them properly, but you can always get a gardener, can't you?' said Helen.

'Or a chap to help with the animals, come to that?' pursued Oliver.

'No, I've never kept an animal. Besides, I think I might grow fond of them and not like keeping them captive, let alone eating them,' lied Peter.

'You're hopelessly sentimental,' said Helen.

'Don't we know it!' said Oliver, laughing unattractively. 'But you're talking rubbish. What my Italian phrase book quaintly calls Bunkum, Tosh.'

Helen moved to Peter's defence. 'Are you going to show us all around inside? Will I find it as enchanting, Peter, as the outside?'

Although Peter had now made two rooms tolerably habitable, the mark of the builders was still everywhere else to be seen – hammers here, fretsaws there, floorboards up, odd heaps of sawdust, most of the rooms merely plastered and waiting for paint.

'I'm afraid builders have been my gaolers far more than animals could possibly be. Infuriating, maddening. They vanish for days, then a whole army reappears.'

'We should have brought you a calendar showing you all the saints' days,' said Helen.

'Oh, it's not only that. They're whisked away on other jobs. Strikes, too, of course.'

'I think I'll be excused a tour of the cells,' said Oliver. 'More Helen's form than mine. I'll keep guard outside and watch the sun go down over the Italian yard-arm.'

The silence of two people, after the falling-out of a talkative third, can seem pregnant with complicity. So Peter thought as Helen moved quietly from room to room, leaning far out of each window, smiling as she pivoted back towards him, her dress rustling lightly. Did he want her to speak or not? He wished that he knew her better. He wished that he was younger and less shabby. Still, there was no doubt he was enjoying it all.

He kept on hoping that the next window, the next doorway, might produce something more dangerously provocative – say, another of those low, husky and unladylike laughs which contrasted so with her otherwise gentle, almost placid, manners.

Helen turned on the tap in the tiny, tiled bathroom. 'So you've got running water? That's good, isn't it?' Peter felt intimate and boxed-in: was reminded for a lightning moment of playing sardines or murder in the attics and cupboards of his childhood home. Oliver couldn't see them, couldn't overhear them, they were safe here. But it wasn't until Helen's hand was on the doorknob that he managed to stammer, his voice high-pitched after clearing his throat.

'Is Oliver happy do you think doing – what did he say – seeing the sun over the Italian yard-arm?'

'He means drinking.'

'Is he, more than he used to be – drinking, I mean?' Peter was delighted if they were about to discuss Oliver's infirmities.

'You don't under-rate him, do you?' – a reproof, if one were to go by the words. But the accent was mild. Peter blinked twice and retreated.

'What exactly do you think we all want to do now?'

'Oliver is going to take us all out to supper.'

'Oh, *dear*,' Peter thought in nanny-like exasperation. He was vexed to be losing the slight initiative which the role of host might lend him.

'I shall look forward to that,' he said.

'Will you? Really?' said Helen, giving him a smile which could be at least remembered as conspiratorial (even if not meant so at the time).

'I don't think I go out enough, really. Do you think I am in danger of becoming a hermit?'

Helen didn't reply; she looked sadly at him. Peter hoped she was not interpreting his question as some sort of appeal for pity, so added abruptly, 'Still, I haven't sat on top of a pillar yet. Or contemplated my navel. So I've a long way to go.'

'And do you suppose, Peter, you will stay out here all the year round? Or just use it as a summer house, like the Italians do? And retreat into the city for winter?'

Peter was touched that she should so often call him by

name in her questions, it made them sound affectionate. Also he was surprised – he didn't know why – by her knowledge of Italian customs.

'I don't really know yet . . .' and funked adding 'Helen'.

'I suppose,' considered Helen, tracing an imaginary pattern with one finger on a window of the room they had now reached (the last of their tour) 'you can feel as trapped in the country, even out here with the sky and those clouds and all those mountains, as in the centre of a city.'

'Isn't there a word for that, for being frightened of the great open spaces?' said Peter. 'Ago . . . Ago . . .' and for seconds they indulged in a happy joint hunt for an escaped word. Peter in fact arrived at the correct answer almost immediately, but didn't say so, desiring not so much to give satisfaction to Helen by letting *her* find the answer, as simply to prolong the delightful exercise.

'Though "open" doesn't seem quite the right word for these spaces, do you think?' said Peter. The most distant range of mountains was retreating under a black stormscreen. Nearer and meaner peaks and ridges closed in on them, in their place.

'It's a nursery-book landscape. You can imagine giants putting on their three-league boots,' said Helen. Peter was flooded with delight that she had caught and echoed his feelings. Really, Oliver had no right to a wife like this. All his instincts about her had been right. He glanced sidelong to see if she would be willing to catch his eye, but she was – not exactly gazing – but looking on the landscape as though learning it, imprinting every changing feature. This pleased Peter almost as much as an exchange of looks would have done. He said,

'And menace, do you feel menace?' But it was the wrong question. Helen laughed her funny, husky laugh and said, 'I'd love to see a storm. I wouldn't be frightened.' Afterwards Peter did wonder whether there might not have been some breath of invitation in the words, some innuendo in 'storm'. But at the time it didn't sound so. The moment of communication, if it had ever existed, had passed.

'It's a great shame you're staying at a hotel. If only my house was ready!' said Peter.

'Perhaps another time.'

They rejoined Oliver. Though his encounter had ended lamely, Peter encouraged himself to feel – especially as he recollected and recoloured their conversation, during a wakeful night hour – that he had made progress and that, by some method he would elaborate in fantasy, he might succeed in his scoundrelly objective.

# 6

Peter had long ago employed a young man with a terror of green fields. The terror had been so great that once, travelling with him from Birmingham to some business meeting in London, Peter had observed him huddling in the corner of the railway-carriage and *quivering* upon their leaving Solihull and gaining the open countryside. Affectation had entered into it, perhaps. He had been a bizarre young man with a taste for polka-dotted bow ties (green ones, curiously). But Peter had been inclined to believe that his fear was real enough. Well, Pan at least never leapt and piped and struck terror through the streets of an Italian city. This memory and reflection occurred to Peter as, with Oliver and Helen, he jostled his way down the steep paved streets of the centre.

Yes, perhaps 'menace' had been too strong and direct a word, but all the same Helen had been quick to sense the threat of the gigantic, inhuman scale of the country. Was this one of the reasons why the modern Italian – even the Italian farm labourer who scuttled in his '500' to and from his tillage or harvesting preferred to live in the gaunt security of a suburban block? The city square was at least comprehensible, even reassuring, even – despite the noise – sobering. Peter acknowledged an acquaintance or two with casual bows and nods. Then, just as he was rearranging the café chairs under the colonnade, he became aware of a clatter, a flurry of umbrellas, a chorus of *ciaos*, reflections of girls in the paper-shop window.

'His' girls, of course. Confronted by youth, Peter felt an urge to exhibit agility. He started to swivel round on his right heel. He disengaged his left hand from the back of a chair and held his right hand up in salutation. He tossed his head upwards, like a horse. The manœuvre should not have proved too difficult. But he had forgotten about his left leg, the calf of which was pressing lightly against another chair. This uncoordinated leg could not, however, fail to be involved in Peter's total movement. Its pressure on the chair increased. There was a scraping noise. Unwisely, Peter groped behind himself with his disengaged left hand, leaving the other one still high in salutation. He was now in the approximate position of a spastic discus thrower. The groping hand continued to search for the scraping chair. It was too late to preserve any simulacrum of grace. A restoration of balance was the most that could be hoped for. Unfortunate Peter! As he attempted to twist his left foot to align it with his right, it snagged against the ferrule of one of the girls' lain-down umbrellas. A skip, both legs in the air, might have still have saved him. Instead, one hand still raised, he began to go down. A few people around put their hands to their mouths. He seemed to take a long time crashing, and entangling with chairs and tables and umbrellas. His falling thought was for the safety of his spectacles.

Shrieks and trills of laughter descended into his ears. He didn't hear Helen. Oliver's hearty accents dominated everything.

'Bit of a nasty tumble, that. Give you a hand up.' As Peter continued to reassemble himself, Oliver went on talking, 'Doesn't do to do too much of that sort of thing at our age. Machinery all in working order? Have a bit of a walk round if I were you. Then a drink. With your new friends. You've not introduced us.'

Peter was so shaken by the fall that he failed to consider its ignominy. However, he was grateful for the cover which Oliver's bluster was giving him. His role as interpreter during the social formalities which ensued also gave him breathing space. Soon, after flicking away enough dust with the back of his hand, he felt strong enough to address a grimace of self-mockery at Helen, who sat placidly as though nothing at all had happened, looking with faintly scornful tolerance at Oliver's heavy bumbling with the three girls. Peter wondered how much ground he had lost with her. Dare he put it to the test? He would annex the attention of his girls (who could easily be made to look as if they were flirting) to see if he could kindle the faintest spark of – no, not jealousy, nothing so strong as that – but *competition* from Helen. Peter set to with a plausible imitation of gallantry, his attentiveness greater than Helen could consider normal for an Englishman. He would risk the possibility that his years made him merely an object of further ridicule in the eyes of all the females.

Obligingly, the girls teased and twittered in Italian: 'Did you go on a gondola when you were in Venice?'

'Did you climb up the campanile? Please answer in English.'

'What do you mean? We know you were in Venice.'

'I don't want an ice-cream, I don't want a drink, I'll just have a pasta, please.'

The prettier one said with a smile, 'Your friend is beautiful,' which pleased Peter. But each time he stole a glance at Helen she was sitting passive and blank, her large eyes settled on the rose-red bricks on the Duomo on the other side of the square. She seemed to have retreated, was certainly not provoked. Then she turned her head (Peter observed the delicious curve of her neck just out of the corner of an eye) and began to look at a man at the next table. Her eyes became less languid, were almost luminous. Peter abandoned his half-hearted attempts at flirtation and followed Helen's gaze. He saw a man with broad shoulders and a curiously domed head of grey hair seated at the next table. Even from the back he gave the air of a creature of power – still but alert – the others at his table competing for his attention while he remained silent. Peter noticed that Oliver, too, threw him an occasional look or two – though much more casually; for his eyes kept on coming back to rove over the girls in jovial greed.

Peter felt that when he had been tumbling he had been the centre of attention, and was now being relegated to the fringe. He was unreasonably piqued at Helen's insouciance, regarding it almost as betrayal. His best hope of regaining some initiative was to bring Oliver into the conversation and attempt to steer it towards a topic which would divert Helen from her continued contemplation of the impressive grey-haired man. This might mean abandoning the three girls. No matter.

'Tomorrow we might all see the frescoes – here, in San Giuseppe,' said Peter.

'Not much of a fellow for frescoes, really. Too much craning the neck. Still, if you say so.'

'Just that – well, they're very unusual. Details that might tickle you.' It was only too easy to echo Oliver's idioms. 'Like dogs licking themselves under the table at the Last Supper.' Peter wondered whether the conversation was now spirited enough to make a bid for Helen's attention, which was still set on those slightly hunched shoulders. However, he was lucky. Oliver was going to do his work for him.

'More Helen's style, really – frescoes. She likes the bits and pieces, too, don't you dear?'

Helen, who had clearly not been listening to them, was now obliged to make a partial return to their group.

'I'm sorry, but who is it he reminds you of?' she said.

'Peter's on about some frescoes he thinks we ought to see. Near here.'

'Of course, if your poor leg will be up to it. Will it, Peter? I'd love to.'

Peter decided he was pleased by this – her first reference to his fall – tied as it was to an acceptance of a joint cultural expedition.

'I'll just twiddle my ankle and see, it's a bit sore, anyway I can always limp if you don't think I'd be too much a figure of fun. Or perhaps I'd look distinguished with a walking-stick?' Peter got up and made a cautious hop or two, one hand on the table, continuing to half-laugh breathlessly.

'No – oh – no – yes, perfectly all right for sight-seeing.' He had imagined that this performance was being followed by a sympathetic Helen. But when he sat down again, and looked watery-eyed towards her (reaching for his spectacles) he realized that all her attention had once again been diverted to the grey-haired man at the next table. He abandoned his spectacle-grope, and panted dejectedly. He watched Helen take a pencil from her handbag, and pass a scribbled note to Oliver, who gave emphatic nods. Would long-distance upside-down reading be beyond him? He would hazard it. He used his elbows to lean up out of his chair as though to reach for an ashtray (not that he was smoking, but never mind). Actually it was a simple note – just two letters in Helen's large, childish script. 'J.D.?'

Peter at once understood (though he could still see only the back of the grey-haired man) part of the reason why Helen had been so absorbed by the man at the next table. He must remind her of J.D.! J.D.! J.D.! The man who, after all was said and done, was still partially in Peter's power! Though why should Helen be quite so fascinated? This might be a subject for delicate delving at the dinner-table.

Meanwhile, Oliver appeared to be making some headway with the girls. Fragments of stilted conversation reached Peter, who was afterwards to remember one phrase in particular. Oliver was saying, 'Given you things to read, has he, the old devil – what sort of *things to read*, I'd like to know. Put me in the picture . . .'

If only Peter had been able to overhear more! But it didn't seem important at the time. Oliver's 'chatting up the birds' (as he would have called it) didn't seem worthy of much notice and, besides, eavesdropping on top of upside-down reading strained Peter's faculty for spying. Nor did Oliver's loud, bumbling Anglo-Italian help matters – indeed, conspiratorial whispers would have been far easier to decipher. In any case, the three girls now fluttered their eyelashes at Oliver, then got up – simultaneously, like birds taking wing – expressed a few rapid hopes for the recovery of Peter's ankle, and swooped around quasi-J.D.'s table. None of them exactly looked at him, but it seemed to Peter's jealous fancy that something in the sway of their retreat suggested that they hoped quasi-J.D.'s eyes might be following them.

'But Peter, listen, he really is very like J.D., isn't he? Almost a double in fact,' said Helen, who must have caught him deciphering her note. 'So spit-image that one somehow felt he would overhear us, in a funny way, if we spoke out loud.'

'Well, perhaps he's English, too!' said Peter lowly and lamely.

'Chap I've a lot of time for, a whole lot of time,' said Oliver, with a snort (presumably referring to J.D.). Peter thought it strange that Oliver should find it necessary to be obsequious at this distance, derogating from his own self-importance. 'Remember that time when J.D. didn't say anything at all? That last board meeting you were at, wasn't it?'

Of course Peter remembered it. In business J.D. was a master of the tactics of motionless silence. (This made his social affability all the more sinister – and *vice versa*.) But it was tactless of Oliver to have mentioned it. Peter, after all, had been the victim on that occasion. Peter said, 'But does anyone actually *like* J.D.? Or do you think that's irrelevant to his scheme of things? One knows of people admiring him, following him slavishly. But *liking*?'

'Oh, I could really be quite fond of J.D.,' said Helen, with her throaty laugh, 'but I'm hungry.'

'Yes, let's eat.'

They walked towards the restaurant. There was nothing coquettish about Helen's movements, nor did she pass any backward glance at quasi-J.D.'s table. Peter guessed that she possessed that ability (associated in his mind, probably from infancy, with both women and cats) for instant *voulu* detachment. It was a gift he envied. For his part, he was suffering the uncomfortable, bilious impression of 'seeing' J.D. everywhere – even the dome of a church they passed recalling the dome of J.D.'s forehead. He took some comfort in the curious reflection that this was better than imagining that J.D. was watching *him*. Or was it? Had there not always been something insulting in J.D.'s apparently genuine unconcern over his, Peter's, actions – even when they were designed to threaten J.D.?

The change to a thundery and still atmosphere made them all edgy. Even Helen's gentle good-nature showed signs of being ruffled by Oliver's obtrusive hostliness.

'It's all on me. The whole caboodle.'

Then towards the end of dinner, just before the ice-cream, an event occurred that was to make the meal one they would remember for the rest of their lives.

# 7

Apart from the unusual mugginess, there had been moments of social prickliness, too, during the early stages of the meal. Oliver had been clumsily prying and probing for stories about J.D.'s early life.

'Secretive bastard, really,' said Oliver. 'No one's got much of a clue about him. Daresay you could tell a tale or two.'

Peter was not to be drawn out far. On the one hand, he wanted to appear knowledgeable: on the other, generous in order to impress Helen.

'I don't think he was particularly happy at home when he was young. Didn't get on very well with his father.'

'Which applies to a lot of us,' said Helen.

'Yes, nothing peculiar about that,' said Oliver. 'No murky details, though? You know, my dear fellow, we've known each other for countless ages. Discussed J.D., too – but never really got down to brass tacks.'

'How daunting you make him sound,' said Helen.

'Simply not forthcoming, that's all,' said Peter. He didn't want to admit to Helen that *he* was ever daunted. Nor was there any reason – well, any real reason – ever to have been frightened of J.D.

'But you say he knows how to keep still,' said Helen. 'I've noticed that myself. Perhaps I shouldn't have said, "knows how". Just *does*.'

Peter had no intention of revealing how much he knew of J.D.'s early behaviour and guilt. The thought of it made him smirk. However, enigmatic smiles do not add to physical attraction. The subject had better be changed. It was exactly at this moment – the smirk in mid-contraction – that the first rumble occurred.

The surface of the red wine in their glasses shivered. A waiter, balancing plates in both hands and looking above tables in a direction other than the one he was going in, seemed to skate a fraction sideways. Everyone stopped talking. A solitary knife or fork tinkled on the tile floor. In this hiccup of time Peter was able to sense both a bewilderment on the verge of panic, and suspended preparation for further action. On whose part, though? The diners'? The earthshakers'?

But, after a second or so, a nervous near-normality resumed, together with a rushing babble of voices. No one quite knew what had happened – indeed, if anything had happened at all. Peter did not even formulate in his own mind the word 'earthquake'. It was as though to give it a name was to acknowledge its reality. Helen's eyes showed fright, she seemed to cower a little and became small; but she stayed silent. Oliver's alarm manifested itself in accusation.

'I say, good God, old boy, look out there.' It was not clear whom he was addressing. He thumped the table and pointed (or rather held out his still-clenched fist) towards Helen and Peter in turn. 'Don't panic, don't panic,' he repeated. After another half minute, everything subsided. Did people feel foolish? Probably not – for uneasy apprehension still showed in the corners of eyes.

A neighbour rustled a newspaper at the next table. The slightest noise, other than voices, was still a little scarey. Peter now remembered reading an account of a minor earthquake in the region a few days earlier. Then he had indulgently speculated to himself how he might behave when hundreds of people (for so it was reported) ran from shops and restaurants out into the streets and gaped at the sky, seeking refuge in the open from the threat of tumbling masonry. He hadn't even in fancy felt able to cast himself as a hero, or as a rescue worker among the debris. But he couldn't demean himself to join the scurrying crowd. So he had decided – still in fancy – to wedge himself into a corner of any room he was in, and curl up with arms over his head. He hoped he would have joined in the panic as little as possible.

The ability to isolate oneself in moments of terror, to stand outside oneself and view one's alien body from above (perhaps from only a very few feet above) – was this protective device conducive to survival? He had recalled an episode of his distant war when he had found himself, on a raw Scapa Flow day, being ferried in the same boat as a sailor in the throes of epilepsy. The contortion and writhing had at first induced in him a certain compassion, even a desire to help. Fortunately this was precluded by ignorance. So he had detached himself from the scene and gazed with unseeing eyes – or, rather, eyes that had ceased to be part of himself – at the mediocre humps of retreating islets, obscured by the wake of his boat. The sailor had choked and died. It had been an emptying experience. Earthquakes might empty one thus, he had supposed. No sublimity. Just a few terror-struck seconds followed by dusty desolation.

Now Peter was not sure. They had endured only the tiniest tremor. He did, it is true, feel a kind of 'lopped-offness' (God was not in his Heaven). But waiting, as in wars or for news of illnesses, for another and 'proper' shock was his principal sensation. He always imagined the worst. He felt a numbness in one of his thumbs, and discovered it was pressed hard into the edge of the table. He hoped that Oliver would propose that they forgo the ice-cream and leave the restaurant, thus saving him from making the suggestion himself and incurring the taint of cowardice in

Helen's eyes. Oliver set the conversation going again by attempting a feeble joke.

'One of the earth's nervous twitches, seems to me! Psychological!'

Helen said, 'My first earthquake, Peter. If you can really call it that.'

'It was a real *very small* earthquake,' said Peter. 'Do you still feel like ice-cream, or not?' he added, with an apologetic half-smile.

Oliver's bluffness showed signs of strain and his metaphors were more than usually inapposite.

'Balloon's going up, do you think?' he wiped his florid brow. 'I'll tell you what,' he went on, 'I'll nip back to the hotel and fetch my camera. Just in case.'

It was a nice measure of Peter's feelings towards Helen that he allowed himself to calculate whether his welcome of Oliver's suggestion (which would leave him alone with Helen) was greater than his queasiness at having now to remain trapped in the restaurant.

'Oliver doesn't feel he's really seen anything until he's taken a picture of it,' said Helen, pleasing Peter by this opening towards another and he hoped longer conversation about the deficiencies of her husband. He wondered whether he dared skirt, very cautiously, the borders of sex.

'I wouldn't have cast him as a *voyeur*, exactly.'

'He prefers to stay on the outside, occasionally looking in,' said Helen, declining the gambit. 'Not like J.D., who enjoys being in the eye of every storm.'

'Extraordinary, we're talking about J.D. again,' said Peter testily.

'Well, the earthquake – your real very small earthquake – seemed to happen just as we were discussing him. Perhaps we were taking his name in vain?'

'I hope he'll stop raining thunderbolts on blasphemers, very old-fashioned thing to do,' said Peter. Helen surely looked and sounded freer – looser – than he had ever seen her before. He was reminded of reading, in his excitable adolescence, of the behaviour of people after volcanoes, of indiscriminate couples lying together on the slopes of Etna (or was it Vesuvius?) in frantic and free copulation, wild with the dionysiac liberation that ensues survival of holocaust – homes and families and friends all around one buried in cinders. Perhaps another slight shake of the earth, just one sudden lurch and a sway of the hanging light, might produce suitably modified consequences?

'Tell me, were you frightened, Peter? What exactly did you feel?' Helen's question struck Peter as evidence of her fortitude, few people (certainly he not among them) having the courage to ask such a simple and intimate question, in the face of another's possible fear. Also he was glad that they were veering away from discussion of J.D. Still Peter did not choose to answer the question directly.

'It happened too quickly, it was as if one's heart had missed a beat.' Helen said nothing, perhaps waiting for more, so Peter ventured. 'If we're discussing reactions, how about your photographer husband?' Too late, he regretted the mild facetiousness.

'What did *you* think?'

Peter considered Helen's question gave him some licence; he would, for the first time with her, say something more than gropings, sentences left in mid-air, instantly retractable ambiguities. A small earthquake could give him cover for a little recklessness.

'Well, it seems – I mean to another man Oliver seems to be bluff and practical and solid, the kind of chap you can rely on on a desert island. But, and obviously you know this better than I can, I saw that's much more of a role than I'd realized, and really he's a lot of imagination which is a dangerous thing to suppress, perhaps, as much as he does. And this imagination made him, I think, more frightened than the rest of us. And, of course, he didn't know at all what to do – though I suppose nobody does in an earthquake. But he'd like to have been a hero, and when he went off for his camera, do you think he was perhaps a little disappointed there hadn't been a part for him?'

'Heroes aren't in your line at all, are they, Peter? I like that.'

'Well, it's been a trying day for me. And I'm sure heroes don't fall down or limp. The gods *laughed* at Hephaestus when he hobbled around an Olympian banquet, serving wine.'

'You're right about Oliver in a way – his posturing. But don't let's discuss him.' This zigzag approach of Helen – the way she first opened and then turned off discussion of her husband – encouraged Peter. He explored the cobwebby crannies of his brain for the correct move in the amatory game. Then it suddenly occurred to him, not without a flurry of alarm, that Helen, too, had begun to play, might be forcing his moves, might even be about to win the game herself. This defensive attitude made him fumble inwardly, and paradoxically emerge from his corner with a more direct advance than any he had so far dared; it was almost *staccato*.

'I should like to talk about *you*.'

'That's an elusive subject, I'm afraid. Not deliberately. But just now, oh, I don't know. Abroad and Oliver and the very small earthquake. I'm a chameleon. Unhinged. Can you have an unhinged chameleon, do you think?'

'We've only a few minutes before Oliver returns,' said Peter, hoping that this remark, if allowed, would at least finally settle the conspiratorial nature of their game they were embarked upon.

'I wouldn't have thought you were a hustler, Peter,' said Helen. He could not tell whether this was rebuke, encouragement or even mild complaint. At least it appeared to acknowledge the fact of his pursuit. Perhaps the evening's events had loosened *him*, too, for he ventured: 'When can we meet again?'

Since Helen did not immediately answer, and could perhaps be judged to look sad, he added.

'Like this, I mean. I like you, you see.'

He felt pleased by the tender sound of this last avowal. He glanced into Helen's eyes, but saw no hint of excitement in them.

'You're sweet, Peter,' she merely replied. That sounded very tame to Peter. 'You mustn't suppose I am . . .' she began.

But what it was Peter mustn't suppose he was never to know, though he sometimes daydreamed afterwards. 'Available'? Too coarse. 'Unhappy'? Too confessional. 'Not grateful'? Too, well, brushing-off. Later he sometimes used this interrupted intimacy to gauge his current mood of regret, yearning, satisfaction, fury or whatever. But now, at that very instant, a second shock rumbled and detonated, more sudden, more violent, more decisive than the first. It rocked them, deafened them, struck dumb terror. Even wiped out Peter's hardy self-consciousness, almost altogether. Only 'almost' because he did think. 'I hope Oliver is buried beneath the falling masonry – what should *my* part be?' while throwing himself under the table. There he could discern, dimly in the confusion, among the moving legs of tables and chairs tugged this way and that, the figure of Helen. 'What an ominous crash to start an affair with,' he was afterwards to brood.

# 8

Towards midnight, Helen and Peter were still sitting up in a stifling but undamaged bedroom, waiting for news or reappearance of Oliver. They were both presentably dusted down. Peter kept on running his tongue over his teeth to check that they were all there, and bending his ankle to make sure it had not been further wrenched. The end, or suspension, of cosmic upheaval, qualified as it was by ostensible anxiety for Oliver's safety, had produced a crop of petty vexations. Pinpricks dotted Peter's consciousness of all their surroundings. The water-taps first trickled and then gurgled into emptiness. Expostulation with the hotel reception had secured charming, slightly scornful and wholly futile promises of attention. Chambermaids, far too polite, did not shelter behind the excuse of chaos but assented to requests for mineral water and vanished lightly down the corridor, never to return.

There seemed to be no progress towards the great Liberation. Peter felt cheated of his fantasy of Vesuvius (or was it Etna?). His determination to conceal the insincerity of his anxiety for Oliver's well-being was so great that he nearly convinced himself, too, of its genuineness. Conversation was spasmodic and stilted.

Peter was aware that he must be looking as unattractive as he felt (fumbling at his collar, his tie awry, sweat behind his ears). And Helen's disarray was floppy, her movements more tired than languid. She hung her neck forward. Nevertheless, sexual excitement did not seem hopelessly far beneath the surface. Perhaps it never can be in a hotel bedroom at midnight, between two people who are not married?

Although softly modulated, the buzz of the telephone by Helen's bed made them both jerk up from their slumped positions. Helen gestured towards Peter with a backhand wave as though inviting him to answer – he was nearer the instrument. Peter blinked at this, pretending not to comprehend the apparent request. He saw no point in incurring any suspicion, as yet undeserved, of bad behaviour. The telephone buzzed again, and Peter leant to rub his ankle, hoping that this adequately signalled his continued reluctance to answer, and that Helen would be charitable enough to attribute his demurral to discretion, or even gallantry – a care not to compromise her – rather than to cowardice. After the call was over he would try to explain that. Helen said, 'I'm scared. It's Oliver. About him.' Peter shrugged his shoulders.

'We'd have heard by now – I mean, he'll be safe somewhere, I'm sure.'

They looked at each other. Peter attempted to impart, into his pale unbespectacled eyes, some expression of the tenderness he then sincerely felt. 'Please, please,' he implored incoherently. 'I'll do all I can, we'll do all we can.'

The third buzz was definitely longer, impossible to deny. Helen removed herself and settled on the bed, resting one hand on the pillow. Peter prepared to overhear, so far as he could, both sides of the conversation. Minutes, so it seemed, of exchange babel ensued – between the hotel, other agencies, and presumably the caller. At last, Helen put her hand on the receiver: 'It's international – what on earth . . . ?'

Then Peter heard a surprisingly clear voice.

'J.D. here.'

'J.D.? Good heavens!' said Helen.

'Yes. You're all right? Both of you?'

'Oliver's disappeared since the 'quake. We're very fraught. But . . .'

Peter semaphored with his hands criss-cross to indicate that so far as J.D. was concerned he, Peter, wasn't there. He was astounded at this fresh evidence of the ubiquity of J.D., this uncanny habit of turning up at critical moments. Proof of scrupulous friendship? Proof of love of power? Whatever the motive, its manifestation was impressive. He was reminded of an incident, in the days of their fruitful collaboration, when J.D. had secured unsecurable seats for himself and his wife and friend at some Covent Garden performance.

'I'd be grateful, really, for *any* seat,' Peter had said.

'Which seats exactly do you want?'

'Stalls would be best. But they're all booked. For every performance.'

'Which evening do you want to go?'

'Well, really, *any* evening. Monday – Wednesday – this week, next . . .'

'Which evening?'

'If it was possible, well, Wednesday.'

Tickets for four stalls on Wednesday had appeared the next day. J.D. had smiled when thanked. 'My dear fellow. Your wishes are my command. Up to a point' ('up to a point' had been a habitual and half-ironic phrase of J.D.'s). Now here was J.D. again, though Peter could not imagine how he had continued to learn, so very promptly, of their minor catastrophe. He picked up further fragments of conversation from the phone:

'. . . assistance . . . consul . . . knows.'

'We don't really know ourselves, I mean here at the hotel, exactly what's happened.'

'Disadvantages in not being on the spot in more ways than one . . . call on me . . . children. Papers . . . success . . . never mind . . . not to . . .'

Peter puzzled a little on the reference to 'papers'. It could scarcely mean *newspapers*.

Helen was saying, in a quicker and more agitated tone than was usual for her: 'Don't bother about that, I'm a bit – well, surrounded – everything will be all right.'

Then Peter couldn't hear J.D.'s reply; he seemed to have lowered his voice. After a while Helen said, coolly: 'It's very kind, very good of you, J.D. I'm touched, I don't know.'

The line died in mid-talk. Helen turned to Peter. She was composed. She said: 'How much of all that did you get?'

Something a little proprietary in her tone struck Peter. Did she resent his listening in? Perhaps that was imaginary, only what he might have felt in her place himself. If there was a nuance of accusation he decided to ignore it.

'Did he say how he'd heard?'

'Something in the news, I gathered. He knew we were here, of course.'

'What was that he said about children?'

'Asking whether I would like him to reassure them, anything he could do. Really very kind.'

Peter was abashed that the existence of her children, her concern for their anxiety on hearing the news, had not entered his head at all. He reproached himself for his self-centredness, feeling the paradox. He said: 'Too late to ring them now – the children, I mean. And shouldn't we really wait for Oliver?'

His mention of Oliver by name, out loud, forced him back to an awareness of his own temporary and ambivalent occupation of the hotel bedroom. He tried to regain his balance by staring round the four walls, hung with reproductions of Gauguins in mean frames, then looked hangdog at Helen. Her smile was not without pity, more than he would have liked.

'I suppose, Peter, you think of J.D. as hard or overbearing. Men often do.'

'Capable of cruelty. Capable of kindness, too. In an impersonal way.'

'So you're *personal*, are you, Peter?'

Peter did reluctantly acknowledge to himself that his ideals – even his generosity – could be thus accused of 'impersonality'. But he was doubly wounded that the attack should be combined with a defence of J.D.

'I've not convinced you that I've cared?' He congratulated himself on not having added '. . . as much as J.D.'

Helen's eyes turned to water, she did not sob, perhaps even 'cry' did not properly describe such a suffusion of tears. Peter was bewildered at what could possibly have been said, or not said, to produce such a full-moon phenomenon. Possibly there was no cause other than tiredness, or fear for Oliver. His hard-to-tap wellsprings of compassion were struck, he held out first one hand then both, and waited for some subsiding of tears. She did not take his hands. What was it he had said last '. . . not convinced you I've cared?' Dared he hope she had taken this as some sort of declaration, and been moved to this display? Continued silence might be his best tactic. He could not think what to do with his hands. He laid them dolefully on his knees, and waited. Women did not lose their attraction when they shed tears – indeed tears in his experience had produced in him surges of desire – but bewilderment was as strong an enemy of sexual arousal as, say, thoughts of the Queen. And bewilderment was his reaction now.

Helen lay face down on the coverlet. Peter wiped his spectacles, adjusted their arms behind his ears with particular care, and considered her body. For his memory's sake he mapped the gentle and pleasing curve of her body. He devoted several seconds to studying the underside of her knees, which appealed to him enough to fan the cinders of his lust. After a while Helen spoke in a voice muffled by her pillows.

'Sometimes I'm amused, sometimes I'm maddened,

sometimes I cry (which is really very silly of me) at the thought of J.D. I never know which it's to be or why. Do you understand, Peter? No, I don't think you do. Too late to explain, too late at night, I mean. I know he can treat people badly, perhaps he treated you badly, perhaps I was a victim, too. But I can't help admiring his particular sort of strength, which puts him out of reach even when he's alone. Is it his strength, do you suppose, or his unpredictable comings and goings or something quite simple like the way he shakes his head, that does that? Puts him out of reach, I mean? I've never sorted that out. It's funny, to be so approachable in many ways, practical ones and so on, and so remote in others. I'm going on. Thank you, Peter. I'm better now, for talking.'

Peter was obliged to acknowledge the weight of his overtiredness. There was every excuse for it. The day had lasted an age. Helen and Oliver's arrival at his home, his tentative passage with Helen by the window, the fall at the café, the earthquakes in the restaurant, the long wait in the hotel bedroom, J.D.'s telephone call. Momentarily he pictured each episode, making it into a solid and separate object, eschewing interpretation. That would come later. Now his eyelids were hard to lift, his limbs felt as if they would severally creak, his silly ankle throbbed. He decided his last intellectual effort would be to decide where to lay his hand on Helen in temporary farewell. Naturally he would have liked to touch her golden hair, or lightly smack her bottom. But they might seem over-intimate, although possible to construe avuncularly. He settled on the space between her shoulder blades, and afterwards (this quite unrehearsed) leant his head down towards her cheek, and said: 'Goodnight. Oliver is safe, I'm sure. I'll come tomorrow first thing. You must sleep.'

Helen murmured back: 'You're really quite sweet, aren't you, Peter?' and he was gratified.

The fusty corridor was now unlit, but outside the hotel

the colonnade was bright with moonlight. There seemed few signs of damage other than some fractured windowpanes. Peter walked slowly towards his car, pondering a small conundrum, even the definition of which he had postponed in the bedroom. He was comparing Helen's 'You're really quite sweet' to him, with her comment about J.D. 'Really very kind.' Was there any difference? Which was better?

But disorderly behaviour prevented his resolving the question. One drunken man slanted and lurched across his path, then another, then a third. They were really and truly drunk, in a shambles, in that extreme crumbling condition, beyond all speech, beyond any co-ordination of movement. It seemed chance, nothing more, that the creatures should tilt and slope this way rather than that. Perhaps leaden feet prevented their becoming totally horizontal? They must have imagined – that is, if they were conscious of anything still – that earthquake was now a continuous state. Clearly drink was *their* means of post-shock release; after all, as common a dionysiac liberation as sexual abandon.

A few more lumps could be seen in doorways, almost imperceptibly heaving as they breathed. The scene was reminiscent of slums in Victorian London. Peter had never seen anything in Italy which so broke the bounds of personal decorum. He approached the old theatre, now undergoing restoration, and barricaded against thieves and vagrants. He glanced upwards to see whether any cracks had appeared on the newly-stuccoed façade. From within came tiny grunts and squeals, which Peter attributed to yet more drunks. The chortles grew nearer. Then there came forward, like operatic brigands from a cave, a shadowy group of four unsteady figures.

Through reluctance to challenge any oncomer directly, the first part of the body Peter was accustomed to notice in any fresh encounter was the neck. He now saw, as the largest of the group became distinct in the moonlight, a throat whose muscles were violently contracting with spasms of half-chortles and half-laughs. Round it was a spotted tie, knotted, loosely hanging awry. Peter recognized Oliver. Perplexity, disgust, irritation, frustration succeeded and overlapped each other. What had Oliver been doing, how had he come to find himself in the half-restored theatre? How could Oliver be so careless, so drunk, so gauche, so thoughtless, so heartless, did he realize what anxiety and distress he was causing Helen? And what a *waste* of Helen!

Then Peter proceeded to 'take in' Oliver's consorts, his capacity for emotion and surprise so dulled that he accepted it as inevitable that they should turn out to be 'his' three girls. He comprehended it all. Well, *some* of it. Oliver had fallen in with them on his way from collecting the camera (incidentally, where was it now, should he try to rescue it and earn a shred of gratitude from Helen?), perhaps found himself running or sheltering in company with the girls, taken them under his capacious protection, then turned to . . . what? He looked at swaying Oliver, and saw no clues. But what did he expect? Bandages round the forehead, speckled with blood? The silence, as they all confronted each other, frayed him.

At last one of the girls muttered out of the shadows.

'Your friend is very polite. A terrible night. He has been looking after us.'

'A terrible night,' they chorused. 'Like the end of the world.'

Oliver said: 'They were damn plucky. No panic. Hardly a sign of hysteria. Their English is good.'

'But how long have you been here, I mean why . . .' Peter blurted. He could not, perhaps did not wish to conceive each link in the chain of events that led from the earthquake here.

'Oh, minutes only,' said the brightest of the girls. 'We told him the theatre was barred. He was saying he loved opera. The night was operatic, it's true, isn't it? The end of Don Giovanni.'

Peter was staggered by the accumulation of improbability – Oliver's professed love of opera, the trespass and impropriety of the girls. Only he and Helen had behaved in character. He said: 'I took Helen back to the hotel. I've only just left her.'

'I say, I say,' said Oliver, with meaningless jocularity. He left his mouth hanging open.

'She'll be relieved to hear you are safe. In good hands.' His eye travelled to Oliver's shoes. The laces were undone. Peter shivered. 'In good order,' he added.

'I must be pushing along,' said Oliver, in the tone of someone in the saloon bar in an English pub. 'Getting back home.'

'I hope nothing is damaged in *your* beautiful home,' said one of the girls to Peter, returning to her formal and complimentary manner of speech.

They all continued to stand still for a few more seconds, frozen as in a *tableau vivant*, each waiting for the other to make the first move. Peter was later to revolve this unexplained, moonlight climax of the night's events. And not least his own role. Could not his orderly and discreet behaviour, his solicitude for Helen (so he saw it in retrospect) be compared with Oliver's escapade? Had Peter triumphed? Had Oliver failed? Or was it the other way round?

# 9

A minuscule rustle woke Peter at first light. Cocooned in his sheets, he lay absolutely still, held his breath and counted. After 30 he expired as slowly as he could, fixing his eyes downward on the eiderdown to assure himself all was still and noiseless. Then he looked up at the roof-beams, checking whether there were imminent signs of collapse. Memory of the earthquake the evening before flooded into his consciousness. Could that rustle be the first harbinger of a fresh upheaval? Premonition of physical disaster (bankruptcy, cancer and so on) frequently clouded his waking moments, emotional complications and practical trivia followed later. A second rustle or perhaps more of a scuffle this time. Were mice about to devour his bedding – he had heard of such cases in long-dis-occupied farmhouses? Before he broke his cover, he would try to determine the source and cause of the disturbance – at least whether it was animal, vegetable or mineral. He decided that it probably came from the stall directly beneath his bedroom. He swivelled his legs to the floor, held his slippers upside-down to disburse any lurking scorpion, put them on, rubbed his ankle, crossed to the window, pressed open the shutters, and looked out on to the vast, impersonal landscape. Then he coughed gently to signal to any intruder that he was in occupation and awake. Realizing that he was still wearing a nightcap, which might be taken possibly as an affectation, certainly as an eccentricity, he removed it carefully, padded back to the bed and placed it neatly under the pillow. He could now descend, though still in pyjamas, to investigate the rustle.

In the porch he picked up an ash stick – just like J.D.'s ash stick, he reminded himself, except that his own was home-made, more rustic. Ineffectual though it might be against scampering mice, it would serve for other enemies – rats, adders, human beings. Was he ridiculous? He looked at the slanting shadow of man and raised stick on the façade of the house and trod cautiously, though not quite tiptoe. Out of the first stall, whose open mouth was still black and unlit by the rising of the sun, there hopped a rabbit. Peter blinked and lowered his stick. He had the instant conviction that this must be Lops, returning from the perils of freedom. That the perils were real was shown by the state of one of Lops's ears, whose top quarter had been torn – or bitten – off. Lops approached Peter and ran around him. After four circuits he sat directly in front of Peter and allowed himself, with only a crouching quiver, to be lifted up and nuzzled. Peter did not bother to upbraid himself for yielding to senti-mentality, for wallowing in the Pathetic Fallacy. It was now his belief – no longer his make-belief – that Lops in some fashion loved him for himself, nor did he now find it fanciful to insist that cupboard love alone could not account for his rabbit's return, his rabbit's soft compliance with his petting.

He shook his head, puzzling to himself how on earth Lops, wrapped in an all-but-airtight polythene bag during his descent into the gulley three days ago, had managed to find his way home. He saw no need to condemn his own betrayal (too harsh a word surely?) in having consigned Lops to the wilderness. Nor did he rebuke himself for his forgetfulness of Lops since. After all, much had happened. He wondered where Lops had been during the earthquake, and pictured his darting this way and that in panic. Perhaps it was then that he had returned to the sanctuary of his farmhouse?

'You forgive me, won't you, of course you will, you do forgive me,' he whispered, with a flash of awareness that Lops's comprehension of forgiveness was more rudimentary than his. Did God ask forgiveness of man, did even a Christian God ask His Son to forgive him? Possibly there was some other divine word, as far above human understanding of forgiveness as his own was above Lops's.

People could be divided into those who found it natural to ask for forgiveness, and those who did not. Take J.D. now – impossible to imagine *him* condescending. To Helen it seemed a more familiar word, her 'forgive me' was still in his ears. Though forgive her for *what*?

Search for fennel and breadcrusts, and consideration of a suitable dwelling for Lops precluded Peter from further examination of the subject. He must not allow his resentment of J.D. to become a cancer; to be eaten up by brooding upon a revenge which (if only J.D. held out a hand) he might just possibly forgo. No – now it was time for Lops and him to breakfast together. In the amity of a meal taken together, they would bury the immediate past.

There are not many boundaries to solitary and unobserved sentimentality, although Peter did realize during the ensuing scene how mockably he was behaving.

A large cardboard carton, of the kind used in the grocery trade for packing detergents in dozens, stood in a corner of one of the half-finished rooms. It contained a few woodshavings and a builder's drill. Peter emptied it, and sprinkled over its bottom the green herbs he had gathered. He placed Lops inside tenderly, not even holding him by the ears. Despite, or perhaps because of, his previous trade connections, the garish red and yellow brand name on the outside of Lops's new home now offended him. He knew where the painter had left a brush and a few tins of paint. He went to fetch them. On his return he was pleased to see Lops settled in and nibbling contentedly. Though still in his pyjamas he thought he would set about his task without bothering to dress. Which colour would he use? Or why not indeed, since he had brought a small selection, give the carton some resemblance to a house? A sort of rabbit's doll-house? He painted in a red door. A white door knob could come later. And should there not be windows?

Peter made no attempt at an Italian façade. The English country-cottage style seemed more appropriate. 'You'd prefer an English country cottage, wouldn't you, old fellow?' he said. 'Sorry you won't have a roof, I could thatch it, well, *try* to thatch it at least . . .' It sounded mean to add out loud, '. . . but it would be too much bother to take off and put on every time I brought you food.' He knelt a few inches backwards and put his head on one side to survey the building operation. Perhaps he might touch in a window box, with an indication of herbs. 'You're such an old nibbler.'

Cosseting was to be Lops's reward for the days and nights in the thickets.

Should he perhaps cut out a window with a fretsaw? To be said against it: (1) a portion of Lops's head and whiskers would look grotesque and Gulliver-like framed by a tiny cardboard window, (2) Lops might contrive to squeeze through it, (3) windows without glass reminded Peter of bombing and catastrophe. To be said for it: (1) it might be cruel to cage a rabbit in a carton, not *quite* so cruel to cage him in a carton with a window, (2) he would be able, if there was a window, occasionally to glance towards Lops and satisfy himself he was still in occupation.

Decision could be postponed. Peter sniffed the paint-brush, and a fresh doubt tugged at him. Might not Lops be allergic to the smell of polyurethane paint? His frantic twitching of the nose perhaps indicated distaste, or even terror born of distaste.

Peter was struck by recollections of a passage by Leopardi;

he padded into the next room, tutted to himself at the piles of books still littered on the floor and then (after carefully wiping his hands and finger-nails) uncovered and opened the book he was searching for. He returned to Lops, dragging his rocking-chair with his other hand. He just had time for a brief recital before facing the major trials of the day. What was it they were going to do – examine a fresco? He hoped, as he found his place, that Helen would be restored enough, and Oliver too deep in matrimonial disgrace, to come on the expedition. He rocked to and fro. He was going to declaim the melodious lines of Leopardi to Lops.

But the reading narrowly failed to elevate or tranquillize him. He did not blame his audience. The trouble was that he was still in a state of dis-equilibrium. His thoughts and vision were topsy-turvy. When he was young and occasionally suffered from bilious attacks, he used to have a similar impression that some small, familiar object around him was blowing itself up like a balloon or monster bubble, blocking all else, growing gargantuan, refusing to burst. He could even turn Lops into a monster, with very little effort. Perhaps Lops was suffering, too.

He had read somewhere that the eyes of some species of hunted animals tended to enlarge, leading them to panic flight when tiny objects – even insects, say – became enormous as they approached. So now, as he closed his book and peeped over the high wall of Lops's new habitation, he supposed he might be turning from giant to supergiant in his rabbit's eyes.

Were men, in whom the growth of sexual desire or fantasy was accompanied by sometimes inconvenient tumescence, more prone than women to such illusions of gigantism? Not *all* men, of course he would not dream of suggesting that. How about J.D., for example? *There* was somebody who seemed able to see each piece of a jigsaw plain, and fit them together (or indeed leave them higgledy-piggledy if that was what he happened to prefer). He could not imagine J.D. so obsessed with one piece of a puzzle, as to lose sight of all the others, and thus to abandon hope of completion. Of course, that did not make him likeable, except to Helen; but perhaps Helen found his strength, his aura of power held in reserve, more of a comfort than an attraction. Was that too much to hope?

Peter bent to stroke Lops, who cowered for a second before responding to his caress almost as a cat might. He ran a finger lightly up and down the torn ear.

# 10

It might have been mere craftiness when on the previous evening Peter had suggested a visit to the frescoes of San Giuseppe. Nevertheless the prospect gave him pleasure, spiced with anxiety. Would Helen enjoy as much as he did the incidental details of the paintings? He regarded this taste of his as an excusable quirk, even if in moods of disdainful self-criticism he did charge himself with running away from – 'shirking' – contemplation of the sublime truths of the major painters of the Renaissance. Perhaps it was a similar timidity that led him to the study of *lesser-*known poets of the Duecento.

All the same, a cat that slunk round the table at Emmaus, eyeing with cautious scorn a sleepy hump of a dog, held his gaze for longer than the figure of the resurrected Christ. *That* was genuine. Would Helen condone this aesthetic humility?

Peter climbed the steep, paved back-alley that led to San Giuseppe, to check that the curator was present before attending upon Helen and Oliver at their hotel.

This part of the city appeared undamaged. It was placid, smoothed over as a sheet of water in dead calm, all traces of passed-over storm erased. A geranium pot, half-emptied of earth, lay on its side under a bench; but it might well have been there for days or weeks. The easy continuance, at least on the surface, of ordinary life after a near-catastrophe (Peter felt obliged to qualify it with 'near' in the light of the morning – perhaps neighbouring cities had suffered more severely) echoed his reflections on the cat at Emmaus.

Peter tugged at the iron handle of a bellcord. Shutters banged over his head. Peter stared up at a grey-haired lady. Something about her seemed familiar. Though surely on his previous visit he had been conducted by an elderly man – her husband presumably? She said, without greeting, 'Today's a feast-day.' 'But can you show people round, are you opened?' She said, 'You're the Englishman, aren't you? *What have you done to my niece?*' To show his incomprehension Peter shrugged his shoulders, spread his arms and opened his palms outward, almost the position – except for the head thrown upwards – of a Crucifixion. 'Wait, I'll come down,' said the beldame harshly. But what niece could Peter possibly have maltreated? Or were *all* Englishmen to blame for the unnamed crime? In the interval, as her clatter grew nearer down the stairs and a bolt was pulled, it dawned on Peter that she had a faint family resemblance with one of his three girls.

Before battle began, as a discipline to steady his nerves, Peter made an inventory of the dark passage that opened up into the interior – a small wooden crate containing a few artichokes and tomatoes, a rusty bicycle and two or three large iron bolts. This exercise served as a substitute for silent counting-up-to-ten, helping give him courage to meet the stare which, he sensed, was fixed upon him. He would have to resign himself to endure a bout of hysteria. But the old lady was dolefully, balefully silent. 'Well . . .' she said at last, '. . . at least you've come.'

Peter said, 'There is a mistake. You must explain. I've simply come to see the frescoes.'

'I want to be told before I send for her parents – the police perhaps.' Peter was at sea. 'But what is the girl saying, I never even knew she had an aunt living here, she has never spoken of you?' He blinked with irritation at thus admitting his acquaintance with her niece. He was rattled. He went on, 'I did see – well, I suppose one of them may have been your niece, I don't know – three girls last night. They seemed all right, perfectly all right, a bit shocked naturally. *Three girls.*'

Peter blinked again, this time at the sudden apprehension that he might already have said too much: that, in the old woman's crazed fancy, he might appear to have now confessed to participation in those post-earthquake orgies which had, indeed, at one time, occupied a corner of his imagination.

All Oliver's beastly fault! But honouring of the ancient code on sneaking, all the more sacrosanct for being an affair between two Englishmen abroad, made it impossible for him to protest his innocence at Oliver's expense. Anyway the girl's misfortune was probably no graver than a bad hangover – some bruise or scratch from the tremor – some verbal impropriety of Oliver, magnified by difficulties of language.

Even while Peter was casting round for the best way of proceeding with the dialogue, he was calculating one advantage that might be culled from it. Oliver had better be kept away from the frescoes. So he would have Helen to himself for their inspection of the Last Supper and Day of Judgement.

'*All right?*' the old woman screeched, raised an arm, then turned aside and spat into a corner. 'She will never be the same again.' Peter realized he was badly out of his depth. The penny had taken a long time to drop. Yet he could not bring himself to spell the word 'rape' in his mind. Even more than murder, this was something done only by other people, to other people, of other classes. The shock of even admitting the idea, buffeted him. It was sudden, overwhelming, a gust of horror which enveloped him in the smells and sounds of the previous night's terror. But although he did, literally, rock on his heels as though he had been physically assaulted he could still make one last, faint effort to pretend that nothing serious had happened. Things could somehow be papered over, fictions restored. He said, 'I promise you . . . please, if you like, tell the girl I am here.'

'She will not see you. What do you suppose?'

From the background he imagined he could hear shuffles, and noises halfway between hiccups and sobs. Peter felt he had strayed beyond the boundaries of his world, was trespassing in another country altogether. Familiar objects grimaced at him, even a dry scar on one of the tomatoes in the crate seemed sinister. Nor was his awareness of his innocence of any consequence whatsoever. He could look nothing in the face. He stuttered, 'But I'm not responsible. I know nothing. Absolutely nothing. You are making a mistake.'

'I know where to find you.'

She slammed the door in his face, and clanged home the bolt. Peter shivered at the seriousness of her apparent accusation. Then he started to walk, without conscious direction, and with every step he walked a little faster. He felt as one feels as running in a nightmare. Running and running, while actually moving not a yard. He imagined that people crossing the road were staring at him, pointing at him, naming him. A greengrocer he knew, hunchbacked, with a pockmarked face (until now a friendly gargoyle of a man) saluted him, and to Peter it was as though he had shaken his fist. Nor did back-streets offer refuge, encounters in narrow places might be more minatory. Gradually he came to realize that he was nearing Oliver and Helen's hotel and had formed no idea how to announce his news to them. First, he must wrench his mind back from its disengaged whirring. He would do this by addressing himself to an immediate question: would a few moments' appraisal of things in a café – or in a church – calm him the better? For solitude's sake, he turned aside into a tiny baroque oratory and sat in the front pew. His nerves began to grow a little (but not much) steadier the more he repeated to himself that he was no malefactor.

One corner of a mosaic Garden of Eden was a favourite of Peter's. Against a cloudless azure sky doves perched on olive trees, a lion (emaciated but not, evidently, hungry) stalked among lambs, a hutchless but secure rabbit nibbled at a clump of grass each of whose blades stood spikily up at the sky. Adam and Eve were sheltering behind a scaffolding, being restored, to the left of the apse. Agreed, it was an inappropriate occasion to contemplate the unfallen state of the world, even if Peter was able to convince himself of his innocence – well, partial innocence.

The brilliant colours, the arcadian simplicity had power to console Peter. He was tempted to withdraw altogether from the affair, leave Oliver to clean up his wreckage, desist from the pursuit of Helen, retreat to his lonely fastness. After all, the girl, once recovered, would acquit *him* of any villainy. He could disclaim without any qualms all friendship and responsibility for Oliver – everything, in fact, but the most passing acquaintance with him. And Helen? She could not welcome a suit pressed under these unsavoury circumstances. *That* was over.

Yes, Oliver could certainly look after himself. Peter would like to see him tussle with the carabinieri (were they the branch that dealt with rape?). They were fitter, stronger, bloodier than Oliver. Good luck to them.

But – and it did come back to this, every time he brought his eyes down from the gold-and-blue mosaics – what exactly would Helen do? She might, he supposed, invoke the protection of J.D.

And J.D.? J.D.'s mordant delight in Oliver's escapade (and 'escapade' was the word J.D. would come to use, Peter was sure) would be tempered only by his evident and close concern for Helen. Peter's thoughts channelled for a minute or two down a familiar groove. 'I will go on nursing my revenge against J.D., this might be an opportunity, somehow.' The feel of the idea! It was like running a tongue over a tooth which ached, relishing the pain and anticipating, with dread, the eventual extraction. Peter's venom was a constant surprise to himself, contrasting as it did with his mild reflection in the shaving-mirror. And so he half-corrected himself. 'Why should I think so much in terms of revenge? Isn't it only my freedom I want? What will be the decisive event – if it isn't this – that will break the tie between us? Couldn't it even be reconciliation rather than revenge? How real is J.D.'s aloofness?'

It was a tribute to J.D.'s force of character that brooding upon him deflected Peter from the immediate horror. There might, too, if one believed in precognition, be an element of coincidence about it. For a swishing noise caused Peter to look behind him. There, sweeping to and fro down the aisle with strong strokes of the broom (surely cleaners were not normally so decisive in their movements?) was the grey-haired man who yesterday in the café had so reminded Helen of J.D. He was wearing carpet slippers. The irony of this twin of J.D. following such a humble and respectable profession pleased Peter and he searched in his pockets for a fairly small tip.

These few minutes' muddled meditation emboldened Peter for his confrontation with Oliver. Only during the last half-kilometre before reaching the hotel did Peter take time to consider Oliver's presumed behaviour in the light of what he had hitherto observed of his character. Coarse-grained Oliver might be; but even allowing for the cover which the earthquake might have given him, could a rape or an attempted rape (of a foreign girl or girls at that) have possibly been foreseen of Oliver? Or could it really be that an earthquake jolted people out of predictable patterns? Or might one look on character as so many layers of paint, each one able to be stripped, uncovering at the end of the series a nature composed of standard psychological in-gredients? He was reminded of Helen admitting that she felt 'chameleon'. Helen was honest. Was that a fundamental part of her character, or could that be stripped off, too?

Then, of course, it was well known that some people possessed – or were possessed by – a number of diverse characters, their identity so separate and their inability to merge so complete that, for example, each character expressed itself in different hand-writing, different voices. But somehow it seemed easier to imagine a strongly contrasting duality – Jekyll and Hyde – than a respectable suburban bully like Oliver 'turning into' a rapist. It occurred to Peter than Oliver might have been encouraged to perform his out-of-key role by finding himself in a half-restored theatre.

More than ever, in the foyer of the hotel, Peter suffered from the disagreeable impression that eyes were spying upon him: even the eyes of a coiffed reproduction Madonna, squinting on the wall above the receptionist. And was he paranoiac to think that the receptionist himself, a smarmed lizard (he darted so, he flashed such thin-lipped smiles) regarded him with brusque suspicion, hostility almost? Covertly, Peter borrowed a newspaper from a stool behind the desk, and tapped it against his cheek and chucked it under his chin while he waited. There appeared to be no answer from Oliver's room. No one had seen or heard of the couple that morning. The receptionist was unhelpful. Perhaps, Peter thought, they were taking a late breakfast capuccino in a nearby café. Peter turned and blundered into another guest – one of those English or German spinsters with long necks, who have survived more than a century of Baedeckers. At least he was no cynosure to her standard type. He retreated to a settee partially shielded by the foliage of a rubber plant, and sat down. To his mild chagrin, yesterday's earthquake had not ousted from the front page the customary chronicle of arson, kidnapping and other variations on the themes of personal scandal and outrage. Would Oliver – would *he* – have such notoriety thrust upon them? Only on page five was the earthquake featured. Even there, their city was far from the epicentre; real damage and casualties were a score of miles away.

Over a lowered double-page spread Peter now observed the agitated entrance of Helen. Agitation he thought he could reasonably attribute to her on the evidence of her swinging handbag – swung petulantly, almost as a schoolgirl might swing a satchel, as though saying, 'bother, *bother*!' under her breath. Not that her clothes showed any sign of disorder. Peter did not usually notice women's clothes, but his fond eyes made an exception for Helen's: her café-au-lait pleated linen skirt pleased him, its suggestion of softness and gentility (almost genteelness) a soothing change, in the present circumstances, from the perfect fit and arrogant correctness of Italian girls' trousers. Peter raised his paper again to hide his face, for oddly he had not considered what, if anything, to say should he first encounter Helen alone. Naturally he would not blurt out news of Oliver's disgrace. Would Helen indeed need to know at all? Suppose Oliver, his misdemeanour unreported, were to leave Italy unscathed, unchased by carabinieri? Though certainly Peter intended to let Oliver know that *he* knew; would not deny himself the consolation prize of that minor pleasure.

Still, Peter confessed to himself the hope of a greater conflagration, and was tempted first circumspectly to ignite it, then heroically to rescue Helen from the flames. Now he would confine himself to reconnaissance. What a pity there was no such thing as *gentlemanly* inquisitiveness! Tender solicitude would be his guise – surely not too unfair.

By energetic rustling of his newspaper he announced to himself his readiness to begin their meeting. The noise served also as a signal to Helen, and Peter preferred that she turn – and see and come towards him – under his surveillance rather than that he should appear to make the first move.

He was pleased to see her agitation calm itself as soon as she caught sight of him. He was so cheered by her smile that he forgot to continue his observation. 'We didn't even make the front page,' said Peter, getting up and backing away from the foliage. 'Things seem to be back to normal, it's as if nothing had happened. A little uncanny somehow.'

'Oh, Peter,' said Helen. 'I am glad you came.'

'Where's your errant husband?' said Peter. He liked 'errant', it gave Helen an opening for confidence, and was mildly facetious, not really critical.

'Making a nonsense of himself in a tobacconist. They haven't got his favourite Condor Cut. Naturally enough. He's sniffing.'

'At least he's back, safe and sound. Did he tell you we'd met, just after I left?'

'He's done this before, you know,' said Helen obscurely. What did she mean? Peter did have visions of Oliver sprouting fanged teeth and turning into Hyde (or was it Jekyll? Peter couldn't remember which was which).

'You mean, *break out*?'

'It doesn't seem to affect him at all,' said Helen.

'What did he do – I mean, last time? On the surface he is such a steady, reliable chap. Does he remember?' Peter thought that people with dual personalities probably suffered from amnesia.

'One can't discuss husbands, don't you agree? Or not – not very much?' This was ambivalent. Put-down? Encouragement?

'Except in practical terms, perhaps. If there's anything at all I can do to help. As I said last night. Though things are different now . . .'

'Dear Peter. You're trying to ask me "What's the matter?" Do you honestly mean you don't know?'

Of course Peter didn't. Helen might be alluding to Oliver's outbreaks of satyriasis, but he couldn't be sure, and the ground was too delicate to tread on. Or was it? Didn't the trouble they were in justify a bolder approach? Peter felt a terrible suspense nibble at his bowels – it reminded him of evenings at prep school before the mornings he was due to be beaten for some peccadillo. Was Oliver already fleeing the country, skulking past frontier posts, were the police rounding up suspicious Englishmen throughout the province? Fantastic dreads flitted across his mind. But all he said was, 'Has – has there been any trouble before? Of a definite sort, involving other people?' He couldn't bring himself to add '. . . and the law?'

'What makes you ask that?'

Peter shied from this again. 'We're lucky, I'm lucky to talk like this with you, I feel I'm nearly understanding.' Then he added, rapidly, 'Actually, there's something I must tell you.'

Helen was silent. Perhaps she had been infected by Peter's germs of suspense.

Peter went on, 'Yesterday night when I met Oliver coming out of the theatre – by the way do you know where the theatre is, we could walk there now and leave a message at the hotel? – anyway I was worried because he was behaving so strangely. Then something was said this morning that might lead to trouble. So in a way I *do* know.'

Peter paused. He was realizing the impossibility of telling a wife that her husband was under suspicion of rape. Oliver was the one to tackle. It was only that Helen was so obviously agitated herself. If they could only share their thoughts, it might help to solve the immediate, practical problem. Peter said 'practical, practical' to himself several times over as an incantation to recall himself to reality.

'It was so out of character,' he went on, 'any character. It wasn't just drink. There were some hysterical girls about. I don't know if he told you.'

Peter paused again. 'We'll walk to the theatre, Peter,' said Helen. 'Yesterday you said you thought my husband played many parts. Tell me the role you think he is playing now. But do understand. I don't want you to tell me anything you shouldn't. But when he came back last night he was a very *defeated* hero. I don't really know if my own worries, such as they are, revolve around him as much as they should. But I'll protect him, of course. Tell me as little as you can.'

They made arrangements with the receptionist and set off. Peter cursed himself for his ill luck. That someone who had fled to the farther side of the Apennines to embrace solitude and look after a rabbit should have responsibility of this kind thrust upon him! But even as he phrased the reflection (gaining time by scratching his head while he walked) he confessed its falseness. His exile, he could not pretend otherwise, was the result of failure, of pique, of romanticism, of collapse of ideas too dimly formulated, too feebly followed, too frequently betrayed. He should look upon this imbroglio as an opportunity for redemption or – less resoundingly but more accurately – an opportunity to become both a hero, and with any luck, a villain as well: he could both save *and* enjoy Helen.

'The little I can tell you is that your husband, probably through combined effects of alcohol and shock – shock mostly, I imagine – somehow managed to upset the hysterical girls I was telling you about. I really don't think there's anything more to it than that. I imagine the scene. An enormous, rather shambly shape looming up in the ruins of a deserted building where three terrified girls are taking shelter. Some incomprehensible chatter – Oliver's Italian, as you know, is only up to railway-station standard. Then a bandage. I seem to remember Oliver waving a white bandage in one of his hands. Perhaps he had been asking one of the girls to tie it round some part. Or offered to tie it for one of the girls, I don't know.'

'But you said something, didn't you, about something that might lead to trouble? How did you gather *that*?'

The staccato of Helen's 'that' made Peter aware that he had already dipped his feet into the water.

'I should have said I know the girls. Well, you do, too, of

course. We met them briefly at the café. They help me with my Italian. I was surprised to find one of them has an aunt here.'

'Yes,' said Helen. 'Of course I remember. Quite pretty, in an obvious sort of way. Too much eye make-up.'

'Well, it seems that one of them lives with an aunt who's the wife of the curator of the church where we were going to see the frescoes. All very odd. An old aunt who practically attacked me this morning before I came to your hotel, made peculiar threats . . .'

Peter felt as if he were lunging with big, clumsy breast-strokes out to sea, beyond sight of land. At the same time he spared a thought to wonder how Helen was taking it. He went on, 'Hysterical nieces seem to have hysterical aunts. Anyway, the old lady shouted at me, accusing me rather wildly, apparently she'd interpreted whatever her niece had said as being about *me*. Peter's friend, I suppose, turning into Peter – quite a natural confusion if you're overwrought.'

'I think you've probably told me enough,' said Helen. 'It's Oliver you should tell now.'

Peter admired Helen's calm. But he felt she *owed* him something, though he did not know how to extract the debt.

'I remember you asked me "Do you really say you don't know what the matter is." Does all this, vague as it is, tie in at all?'

'That would take too long to answer properly,' said Helen. 'Perhaps I will some other time, if you're good.' The almost playful note of 'if you're good' seemed out of tune – Peter took it as a means of declining any melodramatic interpretation of his tale.

He was irritated at himself at pursuing the matter. It was crass, he knew. Still, he did not want Helen to go scot-free: to elude him with such terse grace. He said, 'It's just that wild accusations – denunciations they call them – can be very unpleasant in Italy. *Habeus corpus* is Latin, it doesn't always seem to translate into Italian.'

There. He'd certainly gone far enough.

'You're sure you're not making it sound more serious than it is? It's not the only thing that's awfully disturbing, distressing. Give me a little time to think. We might walk on to this theatre of yours, if we're nearly there and see the scene . . . Then turn back and find my errant husband – as you called him.'

Peter was stupefied by Helen's sang-froid, so contrasting with her agitation in the foyer of the hotel. Helen seemed to sense this, for she said sweetly, 'You mustn't suppose, Peter, that what you say doesn't upset me. Well, like so much in the past few hours. Let's sit down a second.'

They sat on a low wall, and looked over the umber-tiled roofs of the lower town. Helen laughed – still her attractive, low laugh without trace of acerbity.

'Once I was almost sorry for him – Oliver blundered on too far and got quite badly *bitten* by a girl, would you believe it? Oliver pretended it was a dog and made me read all about rabies. Then, silly thing, he confessed when I discovered him reading about *gangrene* in that book he carries with him everywhere – the *Ship's Doctor*. All that was ages ago. He's a fearful hypochondriac, you must have noticed. The first thing he worries about, when he gets into scrapes, is his health. In a way it's rather disarming.'

*Scrapes!* Peter could not imagine how Helen could keep so cool. Obviously she knew a great deal of Oliver's character that was completely closed to him. For example, he might be an occasional exhibitionist. Peter did not know what the Italian penal code said about that. A little stiffly, he said, 'Well, I sincerely hope it will all die down, as you seem to imply.' He took out his glasses and rubbed them furiously, peeved that she would not join him in his terrors. She had not read enough Italian newspapers.

They walked slowly on to the theatre. Disregarding

notices, Peter entered, tugging Helen gently behind him. Three tiers of boxes, surrounding the semicircular auditorium, were wrapped in protective polythene sheaths. Workmen made commanding gestures at heavy wooden beams. In the confident morning air of reconstruction, Peter found it hard to imagine last night's grotesqueries.

In any case, he decided that he himself would not have chosen the theatre for tip-and-run amours. He wondered exactly where Oliver had performed his ogreish antics. The gaps between the bare floor-boards reminded him of gaps in a row of teeth – but perhaps they would not have been visible at night. Or, possibly, might they have egged on concupiscence, as Oliver peeped between the slits down into a black abyss? Didn't Boswell enjoy supernumerary thrills lying on top of girls on Westminster Bridge, staring down between the planks at the Thames running sweetly beneath? And – come to that – might the girl or girls have enjoyed looking up at the *putti* which on the ceiling trailed their indifferent ribbons?

He cast his mind back. Surely Oliver had been laughing as he emerged from the theatre? And the girls had been demure? Shame had probably set in later. Perhaps Oliver had simply attempted to cast himself too boisterously into the role of Don Giovanni. As though divining his thoughts (but perhaps the idea in the circumstances was obvious) Helen said, 'Oliver's too *heavy* to play Don Giovanni, don't you think?'

'He's got a very creditable bass laugh. I'm sorry – I should have said just now, I do admire the way you are taking all this.'

Peter by now had had some time to gather satisfaction at Helen's sharing of confidence with him, even if only about Oliver's absurd escapade of long ago.

'You mustn't suppose, Peter, that *I'm* always good. Sadly enough!'

This confession pumped Peter full of hope, it made his

heart bound. At the same time, he wondered whether he dared ask her to elaborate. He dreaded a let-down. If only he – they – could stay a little longer at exactly this patch, if that wasn't too absurdly timid! Then the horrid thought snaked into his mind that perhaps Helen's falls from goodness, whatever they were, might spring from nothing more than a desire to compensate for Oliver's failings, or even to revenge herself upon him.

He said, 'Were all Don Giovanni's victims virtuous, do you suppose? I can't remember, did none of them take successful revenge?'

'Oh, you mustn't ride that comparison too hard. No, I don't blame Oliver, you mustn't suggest that. But you look sad, Peter. Why do you look sad?'

And with the tip of a finger she tapped Peter on the cheek. It was an intimate gesture, coquettish even, had it not been so tiny and quick. Peter chose not to answer her. He tried to rid himself of the feeling that this was an odd time and place to carry on such a heart-to-heart talk.

'Then your un-goodnesses spring from generosity? That doesn't surprise me somehow.'

But Helen had caught some of Peter's diffidence, she looked down and shook her head and tore a scrap of paper. For the first time Peter wondered how old she was, and wished to protect her. She said, 'Now we'll go and sort out Oliver, shall we?' Peter felt the note was conspiratorial enough to leave his hopes undeflated, and to justify his new carelessness of Oliver's fate.

# 11

They had been out of the shadow of J.D. all the while they were in the theatre. Somehow J.D. did not seem to belong there at all; even at a distance he was too substantial, too changeless. Or could he possibly have been the Commendatore? Peter kept these notions to himself, already once having had his Mozartian whims put down by Helen. But thoughts of him had returned, Peter did not know why, as they walked in and out of the shade of the cypresses which lined the brick-paved way up to the Palazzo – an alternative route back to the hotel. Peter reluctantly acknowledged that J.D. might have made a very tolerable Renaissance duke. He would have enjoyed it. And certainly he was ruthless enough. He didn't care a fig for popularity. But how would he have coped with the tactical problems which confronted them now? Peter could not imagine *his* confiding in Helen. Nor would he question Oliver about what actually happened. Most likely he would simply recommend instant departure. And possibly arrange some huge, anonymous gesture towards the insulted girl: for example, send her the entire contents of a florist's shop. Lavish, absurd, mildly insulting – Peter wasn't sure about that. No. J.D. would attempt to obliterate the incident with silence, speed and scorn. And succeed – that was the maddening thing!

As far as Peter was concerned, the imminence of the forthcoming confrontation made him queasy. His familiar disorientation, suspended during his moments of intimacy with Helen in the theatre, set in again: that is, objects ceased to be neutral and assumed menacing shapes, sizes and life. The Palazzo was arrogant, contained huge dungeons in the roots of its teeth. At least the pair of carabinieri, staring slowly at him as they strolled along with hands behind their backs, were their proper size – but he expected the tread of their boots to echo against the wall far more loudly than it actually did. Waiters serving outdoor café tables at the far end of the colonnade were flies. Whether Helen would sympathize with this distressing (and common?) disease of perceiving things at times of crisis in imaginary distorting-mirrors Peter doubted. Sensible English girls like Helen, daughters of progressive schoolmasters of the thirties, probably did not share the disease. But he might well be guessing wrong, her elliptic intuitions, sadnesses and confessions were unfathomed by him. Peter half-closed his eyes, shook his head to clear it of distortions, and fingered one of the porticoes to insist upon its ordinariness. Then, coming out of the distance towards them he saw a miniature wrong-end-of-the-telescope Mussolini, strutting. It was Oliver.

A wave with one hand, a fumbling in his pocket with another, preceded Oliver's opening salvo of 'Ah, you two young things . . .' He dug a heel heavily in, and swivelled around to walk abreast with them, adding breezily, 'What have you been up to?'

'I was escorting Helen to where you and I last met,' said Peter with oblique assault.

'We wondered,' assisted Helen, 'what part you were playing on the boards. Peter rather thought Don Giovanni.'

Peter retreated in confusion, 'Oh, really, any light opera would do, just that I seem to remember Don Giovanni cropped up last night. Because of the earthquake.' As he spoke he directed sidelong glances at Oliver, partly to detect signs of embarrassment, partly to scan his face for scratches.

There were none. Oliver grunted. 'Hold on a second while I fill my confounded pipe.'

'You're recovered from last night's exertions, I hope,' said Peter, edging back into the fight. Oliver clapped him across his shoulders in expansive cameraderie, 'I've been worried about your ankle,' he said improbably.

Peter was thrown off balance. More and more he felt the absurdity of his task. More and more he doubted whether accusations of sexual misdemeanours against a husband endeared one to a wife. Nor could he believe that if Oliver was even half-guilty he could be so bland. Could not the whole phantasmagoria be erased from the record?

All the same he made one more feeble effort. 'Oh – by the way – you seem to be in some sort of disgrace with an aunt – or guardian perhaps – of one of those girls last night. Perhaps because she arrived home so late. Or something. Anyway, there's a muddle. Probably the old aunt's got hold of the wrong end of the stick. I just thought you ought to know.'

Too late, he regretted vehemently having told Helen – having made such a fuss. The situation was too false for words.

Oliver was saying, 'Some people always do get everything arsewise up. Sorry for the vulgar expression, old girl.' He heaved his shoulder in an unpleasant imitation of silent mirth – Peter did not believe that he was in fact amused at all. One of Oliver's eyes seemed to take on an independent life, rolling upwards in a wide-angled cast, failing to focus somewhere above Oliver's head. Peter thought Oliver a giant Yahoo, unrestricted by normal codes of behaviour and human sensibilities.

By now the three of them were standing, uncomfortably in a loose knot, in the central piazza. Confused chess analogies suggested themselves – Helen as Queen, of course, Oliver as a bluff Castle, Peter himself as a crooked knight. The King? Well, no dukes lived in the palazzo now, so it must be J.D., certain to be the last piece left on his side, round whom everything would eventually revolve, for whom the game was played. And the other side? Carabinieri, the forces of Italian law and order? Peter gave up the attempt to populate the board.

'I won't feel like lunch, or a drink, or anything, till this silly thing's settled,' said Helen. 'Apart from that I can't make any suggestion. Except that I'm sure Peter would go along and hold your hand, Oliver, if you decide to confront the old lady in her lair. I'll just stay quietly here. Don't worry about me.'

Peter was happy to help solve the mystery. It would give him an opportunity to examine Oliver, to relish his discomfiture, and to clear his own name.

However, their errand was not to be. A roll of drums filled the air. A small Fiat with a loudspeaker on the roof drove slowly across the square, issuing a proclamation which for all its stridency Peter was unable to catch. Then a rush of running people swelled and bored out of the side-streets and into the square. Alone, half-skipping and half-walking down the main street towards the piazza could be seen a grinning bandy-legged old man, dressed entirely in grey with a grey top-hat and grey spongebag trousers, twirling a baton. The drum beats grew louder. A carnival float of a tridented King Neptune surrounded by chilly-looking mermaids, was followed by a raggle-taggle band of drummers (some of whom looked bored and chewed gum). Then another float of assorted harlequins, then another of characters whom Peter recognized as from the Commedia Dell'Arte – a lanky black-coated Dr Balanzon, a gibbering Captain Spaventa. Curious, Peter had no recollection of seeing any manifestoes which might have forewarned him of this evident festival. 'Odd,' he said to Helen. 'I'd have expected more in the way of banners, more preparations. Still . . .' They continued to gaze and to be deafened. Very slowly a fourth float trundled in. A young man dressed in a

Roman toga was holding a balloon, painted rosy and green and stalked to make a pantomime apple.

The three goddesses, to one of whom the apple was presumably to be awarded, were dressed (incongruously but surely temporarily?) in capes that reached right down to their ankles. Their backs were turned to Peter. Some presentiment led him to expect that they would be 'his' girls. It would be yet another of those curious brushstrokes which during the last thirty-six hours had smudged the lines which normally divided the real and the theatrical. Guessing seemed to be easy, adjustment bewildering. Peter's father used to say, on occasions when he had taken him to the theatre, 'And what will happen in the next act?' But it was one thing to guess at a dénouement, and quite another to understand what sort of a play one was taking part in – or indeed whether it was a theatrical performance at all.

The goddesses on the tumbril appeared to revolve on some sort of turntable, which perhaps worked on the same principle as those used for swivelling and servicing locomotives. Two of them did indeed turn out to be Peter's girls. The third was absent. Peter turned towards Oliver to observe his reactions. He had taken off the gaudy kerchief from his neck – some rugby colours were they, perhaps? – and was waving it frantically.

Helen, pressed against a shop-window, was – Peter soon saw – observing him rather than her husband. He trusted his decorous conduct made a favourable contrast to Oliver's rumbustiousness. But he was piqued at not being able to explain the significance or history of the fiesta – indeed, anything about it at all, and took out this irritation by a mild dig at Oliver's expense.

'Of course,' he said to Helen, 'you recognize two of the three goddesses – Hera, do you suppose, and Athene?'

'And the third one – that's not the one with the aunt?'

'No. Perhaps she's still recovering. Or . . .'

He was surprised that Helen could remember what the girls looked like – and was struck by the thought that she had never confided in him what, if any, explanation Oliver had given her for his last night's behaviour. Not the moment to pursue that now. Peter laughed with modulated indulgence in Oliver's direction, hoping to convey an amused understanding of Oliver's bullyboy heartiness.

'You give him a lot of rope,' he said, regretting the cliché the moment he had uttered it.

'Oh, he's very free,' said Helen, surprisingly.

Peter made a note that – should he succeed in becoming Helen's lover – they might as a prologue have a brief discussion on comparative freedom.

To Peter's stupefaction, Oliver now began to barge and swim through the crowd – shouldering sideways, shoving aside old women, not caring whether he trod on anyone's feet. His victims shrank back, drew their clothes round themselves and disdaining to glance up at his face, stared down their noses at his stomach. Peter stood on tiptoe on a convenient doorstep and watched his progress. He could not imagine what Oliver was up to. At last, reaching the judgement chariot, Oliver clung to a wheel and – whether or not this interfered with the mechanism – the turntable ceased to revolve. Paris lowered his apple and twirled its strings round his thumb. With a lot of hearty laughter and shouts Oliver attempted to make himself heard above the din. The goddesses appeared to smile and laugh back. After a very few seconds, Oliver sauntered back through the crowd, a victorious smirk planted on his face. Peter grudgingly admitted that Oliver had a 'nerve', far more so than he, but did not propose to give him the gratification of asking what had transpired. He could see that Helen was not going to deign to ask, either.

'Rather brave of Oliver,' Peter said with frank insincerity. 'What on earth do you think he said?'

Helen was silent. Peter went on, 'Casting a vote? Though

surely not a beauty contest to be settled democratically? Do ask him.'

But Peter need not have bothered, for Oliver breezily volunteered on rejoining them: 'Just congratulating them on their turnout.'

'Did you ask after their friend?' asked Peter unkindly.

'Oh,' said Oliver. 'Oh that. Lot of fuss about nothing.'

'At least you will have discovered what it's all in aid of – the whole fiesta, I mean,' said Helen.

'I gather,' said Oliver, 'it's all a rehearsal. Only a rehearsal. The real thing isn't until next week.'

# 12

It seemed inconceivable. These things sometimes do. Peter was lying in bed with Helen for the first time. It was mid-afternoon. A week had passed. The long preliminaries were over, the game had begun. There had been a telegram from J.D. He was in Rome and needed to see Oliver urgently, and Oliver had left for a few days to join him.

Peter had the feeling that his life, which had been in slow motion for weeks before, was now running before his eyes at thousands of frames a second. (Fortunately the conduct of his sexual affairs was not so Chaplinesque). Whether or not his life would revert to a more humdrum pace was a question lurking at the back of his mind, in this relaxed aftermath.

Meanwhile they both lay face upwards, and Peter listened to Lops nibbling next door, and stared at the wooden beams above his bed. Flying ants were attacking them, and a few small catkins of sawdust had descended on to the coverlet. Peter was just at the stage of asking, 'When did you *know*, for the first time?' But Helen was turning out not to be a great conversationalist in bed. She was likely to counter such questions with '... and you?'

Peter had laid a bet with himself the previous night whether, in the aftermath, he would lay his head on Helen's shoulder or vice versa. The softness and gentleness of Helen led him to hazard the latter, his own self-confessed weakness the former guess. At least he had been pretty confident that they would not turn their backs on each other.

But Peter was unable to pretend to himself that his imp of detachment – of defensive self-observation – had by any means yet been routed. Their intimacy seemed still very incomplete. With the underside of the big toe of one foot he rubbed his enfeebled ankle; such small physical actions (like picking his nose, but he would not have the effrontery for *that* on this occasion) helped him to pave the way for further questioning. He could not help feeling that Helen was in bed with him partly, or even mainly, because she pitied him. So he was not flattered nearly as much as he would have wished. Helen had been more yielding than hungry, more dear than savage. Her passion had been bridled and decorous . . . well, almost disappointing. She had allowed everything, encouraged nothing. Even the prelude to her orgasmic upheaval had been voluptuous (certainly he must not be too critical) rather than violent. Although he would have liked to pursue her down the tunnel on the subject of pity, he was fairly sure it would be bad manners and bad policy to do so now.

Peter rebuked himself for these glimmers of disloyalty and made a resolution to let tranquillity fill the air. He decided to compose a list of ten beatitudes, counting them off on his fingers beneath the sheet.

He started his silent recital by lifting himself and looking at Helen's eyelids:

1. I am glad she does not use eye make-up extravagantly like Italian girls. I shall kiss her eyelids gently. I hope I am not bristly.

2. I am glad she does not smoke in bed.

3. I am glad she is not inquisitive about me just at this moment, though I would like to ask her some questions soon.

4. I am glad I shall be able to tell her nearly everything.

5. I am glad she is ever so slightly sluttish, otherwise she

might be critical of things like that fretsaw on the floor.

6. I am glad my age excuses me from an immediate return to vigour (though I tell a lie there: really I should *not* allow lies, I should uncrook the finger again, I must be honest).

7. I am glad Oliver is not going to return for two whole days. (I wonder where he is now? What is J.D. saying to him?)

8. I am glad J.D. is exorcized here and now.

9. I am glad Helen will be going home in the not too distant future, and will not be an encumbrance in my life.

Peter was so displeased by his last thought that he cut short his catalogue, and looked out of the window, away from Helen. At this rate he would soon be noticing tiny physical blemishes – unless he was very careful – like the faint down on Helen's upper lip. He imagined to himself that there were two djinns, called Lust and Tenderness, one of whom he would try to conjure up in order to banish the third and *evil* spirit which was tempting him to 'disengage'. He decided to summon Tenderness. Clasping both hands behind his head, he murmured, 'I simply can't get over Oliver leaving us like this, it's incredible. I mean, I can't get over being *properly* alone with you. Do you feel we're, not exactly linked, but hinged to each other? So we'll go on revolving and depending on each other, only squeaking or squealing if we're not lubricated properly with enough loving?' 'You talk too much,' said Helen. 'The thing is true now as it is, and *really* that's all that matters, Peter.'

This intimation that Helen herself might be prepared to look upon their affair as a temporary phenomenon irked Peter. 'You just *said* that,' said Peter, resting an elbow on his pillow. However, that sounded obscure, even to himself, and a bit sulky. 'I mean that can't possibly be all for me. There's so much I want to ask you and know for one thing.' 'Sex doesn't go with inquisition, darling,' said Helen. 'Well, not unless you are a – what is it? – a masochist, and I somehow don't think that's *you*.' Peter thought this could be construed as an invitation to further exertion. Perhaps he would lose most of his self-consciousness again, and recover his lust, if he kissed Helen greedily. But it might be better if he waited a little longer. Returning his head to the pillow, he entered on a rambling discourse: 'I suppose – I'd like to go on a tiny bit more if you don't mind very much – that in the middle of one's life – after all, the traditional time to lose one's way and get stuck in thickets and so on – approaching illnesses and deaths to contemplate – the great consolation is moments of stillness' (Peter stressed 'moments' as a slight riposte against Helen). 'Moments when you feel neither trapping nor being trapped. Perhaps the first part of one's grown-up life consists of hunting, and the end part of being hunted. A gloomy way of looking at things, I agree. But just lately I've been passing through a bewildering stage of not recognizing which part of life I was in. Not helped by solitude, of course. Something you said the other evening about being a chameleon made me think you might be a victim, too – have the same sort of feelings yourself. Anyway, all that doesn't seem to matter just now, as you say. We're together – I'm sorry but the old clichés refuse to be put down – on the top of a mountain pass, no longer going uphill, nor yet going downhill. A sort of magic period of betweenness.'

'There you are,' said Helen. 'You really do talk too much. But don't, Peter, don't. You make me feel guilty.'

'Guilty?' started Peter. 'I don't understand.' And Peter really couldn't fathom this remark. He vaguely supposed that she must be referring, in some roundabout way, to her adultery. Much later on, it was a crumb of consolation to him that she made this indirect confession to him when she did.

'That's terribly unfair, when you make me feel so happy,' went on Peter, blinking. He turned towards her and, fixing his eyes on one of the larger freckles which adorned her white shoulders, imprinted it on his memory. By means of such close inspection he hoped to reassure himself of the reality of his situation, stimulate his desire, and form material for future fantasies. But wasn't he being too hard on himself? He really was enchanted by the pallor of her naked shoulders, and the line of her shoulder-bones. He bent to kiss her just above a breast, folding back a piece of the sheet. It passed through his mind – but only as a lightning thought, not serious enough to lower his rising ardour – that he would be more aroused if his sheets were of crisp linen instead of nylon. Perhaps he was a Nurse Fetishist? – though he saw no grounds for self-recrimination in that. Nurses were splendid. He nuzzled and sucked at her breasts. Now it was time to gaze again at the whole length of her, starting with an examination of her ankle, whose exact shape he had not kept clearly enough in mind. He lifted the sheet and felt, rather than saw, Helen smile.

For once he was not depressed by the knobbly appearance of his knees, the white skin and straggly hairs of his legs. The whole *ensemble* looked beautiful, against all odds. He sniffed casually, relishing the warm melange of smells (an action which represented a rare abandonment of self-consciousness). Soon afterwards he was able to surrender himself to satisfactory lust; and, at least in his own eyes, performed strongly and thoughtfully, before succumbing to an access of tenderness. After a decent interval he said, summoning back processes of rumination in an entirely relaxed way, 'I have never understood the *post-coitum triste* thing at all. You make me very happy, you make me very fond.'

Helen had said nothing for ages. He would copy her silence. But a swarm of trivial distractions, banished during the last half-hour, returned though still keeping decently on the horizon. A builder (he presumed it was a builder) trampled on the gravel outside. He felt a craving for an egg sandwich, only an *egg* sandwich would do. Pins and needles pricked and numbed a leg which he was unwilling to move, for fear of disturbing their stillness. And Lops nibbled intermittently next door. This nibbling irritated him like the drip of a tap, and finally punctured the many-coloured bubble in which he had persuaded himself they were both floating. It was time to get up. After fetching the egg sandwich and anything which Helen might require, he would enter on another round of questions and answers. She had used the word inquisition, but surely he could now be allowed to delve a little into her feelings? He even felt strong enough – emotionally – to enquire into her feelings for J.D.

# 13

'But how did you ever come to be a victim of J.D.? As you said you once were?' asked Peter.

'That's all remote, and yet . . .'

'You feel free though now?'

'I feel released, yes, liberated. Thank you, Peter. (Sorry, I shouldn't have said thank you – please forgive me, Peter.)'

'Free's too solemn a word, I agree.'

'And liberated too trivial? You mean, I've not flattered you enough, Peter?'

'No – I was agreeing that freedom means, includes, implies borders and confines and fences; it's knowing and accepting them – working within the borders – that makes one free.'

'You're being too philosophical. I'm very fond of you, attracted by you, you know that, Peter. I suppose anything more would be dangerous, and break down the fences you speak of – some of them useful, good fences.'

'Tell me, when was it ever like that, for you? Not, of course, if you'd rather not.'

'Once you have betrayed, you can't have freedom. That's a sort of sad sense, is it what you mean to say, too, Peter?'

Peter would much rather not even have skirted the topic of betrayal, awakening as it well might any guilt Helen might have for her adultery. He began to hope – they were still lying in bed – gently to turn the conversation towards memories of innocence. He recalled the cover of a picture book of his nursery: a small girl kneeling to pluck a cowslip in a paddock. (Was there a pony in the corner? He couldn't remember.) That sort of happiness. J.D. could wait in the wings while they played in Arcadia. And so could Oliver.

The veering quality of Helen – but perhaps it was true of all women? – disarmed him. But it was most perplexing, too, he considered, scratching his ankle with a toenail. When one wanted to tackle difficult subjects (like Helen's relationship with J.D.) she turned aside. When one wanted to bask in the calm, she reminded one of storms ahead. One could only come zig-zag to a point. Or was this another facet of his own disorientation – like his confusion between active and passive?

Peter stopped scratching his ankle, lay absolutely still and decided to give Helen a glimpse of the distant days of his own absolute innocence. 'I can remember,' he started, 'a photograph of me aged four being taken for a ride by my father on an amazing wooden contraption he had built himself. It was six feet tall, as tall as him, and one sat in a wicker basket above a single huge wheel, cartwheel size (though I don't think it *was* a cartwheel). He used to take me on picnics in it, he would push it everywhere, along overgrown wood-paths, so one sat high above the brambles. It was exciting but frightening being so high up, level with my father's head. I trusted my father absolutely, he was the only person I ever did trust absolutely, without reserve.'

'And did he ever let you down, did you ever fall from your bicycle?' asked Helen.

'Monocycle, really,' corrected Peter absently.

'I think the sad thing is that one goes through so much of one's life without really trusting,' he went on. 'Of course, it's because of making use of people. One can't really trust people who make use of one: so obviously – it follows – one can't trust people whom one uses, either. Not just in business either. In marriage, even in friendship, you can easily slide into the used/user thing. But now, with you, it's different. Not just – please agree not just – because we're sort of suspended in an isolated bubble of time.'

Helen didn't answer, but trailed some of her long hair affectionately across his shoulders. After a long time, seeing that Peter was waiting for her to speak, she gathered herself to say, 'I think women are more reconciled to being used, perhaps something to do with sex. I'm not sure if I agree anyway that love's quite so linked to trust – not necessarily linked – as you imply; to me it's so much more a matter of becoming a part of someone else, flowing into him freely and uncomplicatedly.

'What is true is *us* here and now; and that is true, absolutely true, I promise. Not deceitful one bit. Whatever's happened before, or may happen later. Don't harp so on trust – that's a puritan virtue, noble and puritan. I'm not either of those, I'm afraid, don't really want to be.'

'Trust,' said Peter uncertainly. 'Yes, perhaps it is just a nerve of my decayed religious tooth.'

'But are you religious at all?' asked Helen. 'It's shameful how little I still know about you.'

'*Still!*' Peter was a shade nervous about this implied intention of Helen to enmesh him further. But he felt expansive and relaxed enough to reply: 'It's hard to shed it altogether. I suppose that now I'm really agnostic or liberal humanist – if you must have a label – with an uneasy and intellectually reprehensible sense of something Awful brooding in the background. Does that sound too feeble? I don't rely on anything, or worship anyone. I think I *used* to. When I was a child I can remember singing Mrs Alexander's hymns and thinking Christianity was very comfortable, singing:

> There was no other good enough
> to pay the price of Sin
> He only could unlock the gate
> of Heaven, and let us in

I used to walk along, kicking stones with my new shoes on the last day of holidays. My mother said I was out of tune.'

'And what sorts of gods have you constructed since – I mean, in between then and now?'

'You're implying I'm a weak character who needs gods. Well, I suppose I am. Yes, in a way, that was my downfall. Setting up and admiring demigods I didn't really trust. Like our mutual friend, J.D. To be honest, it was J.D. who actually *ran* the business in most practical ways. Often I felt little more than a figurehead. *My* name, of course, it was my family's business. Anyway, I raised J.D. up, then tried to get the better of him by underhand ways.'

'Underhand? On J.D.?'

'Well, yes. Actually, yes. Though you mustn't suppose I like myself for keeping incriminating papers (that's what they're called, aren't they?).'

'But I don't know about this. What incriminating papers?'

'Oh, things that don't show J.D. in a very favourable light. I just keep them, that's all.'

Peter was aware of the danger of the unattractive laugh, and hoped he had avoided it.

'Not use them? Not even think of using them?' Helen asked.

'Only when I'm bitter, and seem to *make* bile, manufacture it. Not now, least of all now.'

'Tell me about them. I'm curious. Well, that's honest, isn't it, Peter? And, as an old friend of J.D. you must see . . .'

'And then you'll tell me about being a victim of his?' Peter felt, ignominiously, as if he were engaged in a schoolboy swop.

'Oh, that,' said Helen. 'You must have guessed, Peter, I had an affair with him.' It was amazing how casually she said it.

'Oh, that,' Peter echoed, trying to keep his intonation neutral (and indeed he could not decide exactly what he did feel).

'And Oliver in all this?' Peter asked, partly in ignoble anxiety for his own skin (just how complaisant had Oliver proved on that occasion?).

'Oh, he doesn't know, never knew,' said Helen. 'Oliver almost doesn't count in that sort of way.' Peter was shaken by the flatness of her voice, revealing a capacity for unkindness he would never have guessed in one whose attitudes, gestures, voice had until now seemed so gentle. Helen continued speaking more softly.

'I'm sorry, I simply don't care for him any longer as I should. I just look after him, get him out of scrapes. That's why you needn't be jealous of him, ever.' 'Darling Helen,' said Peter uncertainly. 'Perhaps it would be better if we didn't discuss Oliver. You said yourself . . . husbands . . .' Peter's sentence trailed away.

But evidently Helen thought she had better be done with Oliver. 'That's why, you see, I wasn't really too concerned over these ridiculous goings-on with your Italian friends. Anyway, I knew it wasn't serious.' 'What was it all about, do you suppose?' asked Peter, feeling once again that they were really just circling round the subject of J.D., and would shortly have to return. 'Oh, Oliver's little sin is very much what you'd expect – fumbling and fondling, he hasn't the courage for more.' Suddenly, Peter felt sorry for Oliver. He would have liked to give Helen a cue whereby she could restore herself, in his eyes, as a completely gentle, compassionate creature. He couldn't think of one. 'Anyway, you don't suppose there'll be trouble – I thought of the police, God knows what.'

'I see I must explain a little bit more about Oliver,' Helen said. Although the tone was mild, even loving, Peter felt chill at the actual words. He preferred her earlier reticence.

'You talk of him as such a defeated person,' said Peter. 'I can't think he is, altogether.' Peter felt that some expression of sympathy with the man he was betraying was in order. Also he actually *wanted* to take Oliver's side – it seemed some sort of voluntary payment in kind for the loan of his wife. 'It's sad,' said Helen. 'Somehow I think of him more as an "afterwards" person, someone to whom everything's happened already, and who's got absolutely nothing left.'

'And anyway, who defeated him?' went on Peter.

'That was J.D., too.'

'Because of your affair with him? I'm not jealous, don't suppose I am,' said Peter, trying to wound Helen a little. It was ridiculous, they seemed to be on the verge of fighting.

'Oh, no, before that,' said Helen. 'I had an affair with J.D., I'm afraid, *after* he'd succeeded in destroying my husband, rather than the other way round. By that time, I'd come to see Oliver as a shell. Mostly it was the way he gave in to threats, whole series of threats. In the end, there seemed to be nothing there.'

Peter was shocked by Helen's descent to frankness. 'What sort of threats did J.D. make?' he asked. 'I mean, I can remember J.D.'s ascendancy over Oliver, even *trampling* on him in business, but I can't remember any specific destructive acts.'

'I'll tell you one,' said Helen. 'He told Oliver that his price for agreeing to some deal or bargain – it really doesn't matter what – was me.'

'But how did you find out?'

'That's just the point, Oliver told me, and asked for advice. Oliver *telling* me was the ruin.'

'How on earth did he put it, can you remember?'

'It was the fact of his asking my advice that – as I say – seemed to finish his destruction. He stood there saying J.D.'s an extraordinary chap you'd never believe . . . of course, two sides to every question . . . told him it was out of the question, ha ha. It took ages.'

'And what did you say?'

'I laughed at Oliver. Actually I was amused, in a ghastly sort of way. I remembered that Frenchman who said, "Les cornes, c'est comme les dents. Ça fait mal quand ça pousse and puis l'on mange avec." Oliver looked grey when I repeated that to him. But I think he was relieved I seemed to have taken it so well.'

How ludicrously ill-timed Peter's exploration of his own age of innocence now seemed! Quite different genii appeared to have been released in Helen. Such coldness towards Oliver was forgivable, of course, in the light of his character and conduct. Nevertheless it seemed an aberration for her. But at worst the hardness might be a cancer which could be removed with loving care. Peter caught himself up at this. Why ever was it his duty to soften her towards her husband?

Just that it was a side of Helen he had not suspected, that's all. Really, though! It seemed ungallant, even if it were possible, to undertake such a drastic revision of her character whilst still lying down. He didn't want to go on talking, didn't want even to admit to himself his burgeoning accusations. He glanced at Helen's hands, not daring to look into her eyes. No – they were the sort of hands usually described as 'sensitive' and delicate (why? Is there in truth any correlation?). But oh, however could she possibly suppose that her revelation of unfeelingness towards Oliver, so much in contrast with her previous gentle resignation, was a happy epilogue to their love-making? The kindest explanation was that Helen imagined her confession relieved him of obligation to feel guilt.

Saddened and unsettled, he said, 'I'll get something to eat. There's not much, I'm afraid.' In a corner of his mind he thought food might assuage Helen. They had had no lunch. Their meals were out of joint. And indeed she seemed to feel the need to change direction herself, for she smiled and said with a return of sweetness. 'Thank you, Peter. I've said enough. You're very good to me, *for* me. But don't forget, I still want to hear about those papers.'

# 14

On his bare feet, poking among the sparsely-stocked shelves of his kitchen (there seemed still to be more sawdust than food on them) Peter whistled tunelessly. He was not cad enough to admit to feeling a pleasant sense of conquest – or, perhaps more accurately, he was too much of a hypocrite to acknowledge to himself that the feeling did nevertheless lurk in the back of his mind. He felt immensely refreshed and invigorated. When he looked at Lops, instead of communicating with him as another suffering, imprisoned creature like himself, unable to take freedom when offered it, he was masterly and casual towards him, merely tossing into his house a few yellowed outside leaves of lettuce, without bothering to add a single word of endearment.

It began to *enlarge* him that he had Helen to look after – for a while anyway – and that she was neither so perfect nor so gentle as she had formerly seemed. It took him out of himself (as his old Nanny would have said), it did him the world of good, it brushed away the cobwebs.

A different room, a different posture, respite from immediate physical contact with his new mistress – it was surprising how quickly these produced a favourable change of mood.

Peter turned a chicken carcass over and over, inspecting it. There was enough meat on the breast for Helen and two perfectly good, untouched wings for himself. He ate a sliver of the crinkly skin in his fingers. Never in his life had he felt less like a victim, more robust, readier to enjoy everything the world could offer him. Not indeed that chickens had ever populated his change-of-role delusions, chickens were the last animals – less likely even than most vegetables or minerals, come to that – to assume menacing *personae*. One did not imagine chickens larger than oneself, being chased by chickens with carving knives, having one's neck wrung by them. One did not even feel sorry for chickens, not even those forced to live their brief, profitable lives in batteries, listening to music. But perhaps that was just a failure of imagination? And how about baby chicks at Easter? Suppose chickens did have sensibilities, grew fond of other chickens, even of people? No, stop, nonsense. He gave a last chew, swallowed and wiped his fingers. He told himself that he was freed, at least for the time being, of this type of disorientation disease. He would be a proper carnivore now, and attend to chewing.

A shaving mirror on top of the hood of the grill caught his eye. He decided to move it somewhere more suitable. Helen, for all her nonchalance about surroundings, might well think this too slovenly. Nor did he wish to mislead her into believing that he wanted to become dependent on her housewifery. If anything, in his new mood of confidence, he wished to take care of *her*; indeed, her strange outburst against Oliver – he thought he could say 'against' – had now provoked a desire to pamper her back into softness. Out of passing curiosity, rather than vanity, he looked into the mirror. Did it show any signs of confident New Man? He turned it over to its magnifying side, and put on his spectacles to examine his face more closely. He focused the mirror on his lips, and drew the back of a hand across them, to wipe away the suspicion of a scab. Then he opened his mouth, and bared his teeth at himself (the molars were certainly yellow. He hoped that Helen had not gazed at him as close up as he now saw himself, especially as *she* did not suffer from merciful short sight). And the skin of his neck was not unlike the skin of a chicken.

To reassert himself he wrenched the wing into two and put one half into his mouth – a manœuvre he managed without letting go of the mirror. He clamped the bone firmly between his teeth, as a dog might. His mouth was now stretched, his eyes narrowed, the lines formed by his nose and the wrinkles on his forehead formed the shape of a diabolo. The expression reminded him of the grimace of a Japanese samurai. He exaggerated it still more, and clenched his teeth still harder.

It wouldn't be prudent, even if it were possible, to crack a chicken bone using his front teeth only. But he chose not to allow himself to nibble at the flesh on the wing until he had demonstrated his prowess to himself. So he switched the bone to fix it between the last two teeth in the left-back of the mouth, pausing for a frozen second or two to gaze at the reflection of his now bulbous and flushed cheek. It reminded him of a pantomime Roman emperor's.

Then he drew in nearly all his breath preparatory to major mastication, placed an elbow on the shelf, adjusted the mirror again, held his breath, and clenched his jaws with all his strength. There was a sharp retort and a satisfactory if perhaps excessive shivering of bone. (How wise to deny dogs this pleasure!) His tongue explored the débris. Suspicion flooded him that not all the splinters and knobbly fragments were chicken-bone. His tongue began to sort out the bits and pieces and shunt them over to the other side of his mouth; he held the mirror even closer to his mouth and peered into its cavernous gloom. Then his tongue returned from its shunting mission and proceeded to explore and dig and glide like a fat, short snake. There was no doubt of it: both methods of observation confirmed what might so easily have been predicted – he had broken a tooth.

No euphoria, it is safe to say, can survive the sudden destruction of a tooth. That most distressing of middle-age nightmares, the mouth chock-full of teeth breaking, crumbling, disintegrating, was coming true as he stood in front of his new kitchen sink, wearing his long, shabby dressing-gown. He laid down the mirror, put a hand to his mouth, pinched by suction his cheeks together, and regurgitated bit by bit the distressing jumble.

Once upon a time, a thousand years ago, mask clamped over his mouth and nostrils, he had sought to defy the dentist's gentle gas by gazing through the sashed window at a lark soaring higher and higher and higher. That was the first time he had swirling thoughts of his soul leaving his body, aspirations incongruous with his gawky adolescence. Returned to consciousness, one tooth less, he had felt cheated, flat and earthbound. Memory of this early milestone of his youth (if extracted teeth could be so called) made him feel a very old and tired traveller indeed.

But his immediate question was, should he tell Helen? To do so would run the risk of forging a new link in a chain of petty obligations, hopes, anxieties. It would provoke her pity. Yet what sort of figure did he cut in Helen's eyes anyway? For one so introspective, it was extraordinary how little time he had devoted to imagining what was her picture of him. To judge from Oliver, Helen might have a propensity for lame dogs, or those who would in the future become lame. Had he, horrid thoughts, already more in common in her eyes with Oliver than with J.D.? He could not suppose that the little he had to offer, whatever it was, would be enhanced by this disastrous loss of a tooth.

He made tepid a small saucepanful of water, tried without success to find an antiseptic and 'rinsed out', indulging in more fleeting memories of dentists' visits. Then he examined again his now craggier and less hospitable range of teeth. The new crenellation looked and felt to his tongue very jagged – in particular one peak which would certainly need demolition.

To cast more light upon the gloomy scene, he stood with

his back to the window so that the mirror reflected, along one of its sides, the world outside. This, too, was undergoing an unpleasant transformation – here, long tendrils of mist curling upwards; there, slabs of mist brooding over gulleys. Also, it was suddenly getting cold.

An immediate retreat to the warmth and comfort of bed, obvious palliative of this melancholy conjuncture, was overdue. Throwing away the offending chicken wings, he succeeded in assembling without further catastrophe, a tray of ham, bread, salad, cheese and wine. He padded into the next room, extracted a blanket from some newly-erected shelves, draped it like a Red Indian over his shoulders, and returned to the bedroom to see Helen lying with her back to him, her face to the window. He coughed gently, like a stage butler. Helen turned round towards him. She was crying.

Peter then pushed chin down on chest and gazed at Helen through the interstice between his spectacle-top and eyebrow. The look was solicitous, but not without an element of irritation and even of reproach. It was hard, just as he was about lightly to touch on his own troubles, that he should have to sympathize with Helen. Before he had time, however, to approach closer he heard a scrunch, several scrunches, on the gravel outside. This time it could not be the builders – they had left ages ago. Callers? Hunters? Unwelcome whoever they were.

He cocked his head, ran his tongue over the jagged tooth, half-shut his eyes and froze. The scrunching ceased. Now there was a murmur of voices. Helen started up, stared at him and clutched the top sheet to her breasts in a gesture familiar from the cinema. Peter put a finger to his mouth, laid the tray very slowly on the floor, and tiptoed over to the half-shuttered window down one side of which, when he was within an arms-length, he backed, peeping out. He did not care if he now looked more like a pantaloon than a butler.

The murmurs rose and fell, Lops scuffled in his cottage-hut next door. Peter squeezed his toes in fright. The murmur resumed and Peter could swear that one of the voices at least was English. Surely it couldn't be Oliver's? 'Liketove-shown . . .' Not Italian. Peter was rigid.

Why had they heard no warning knock? (Of course, there was no knocker. The bell was disconnected, there was no electricity.) Perhaps they would succeed in lying low, remain undetected. Was there a key in the back door? Where was the car? Where were his clothes? Helen's clothes?

Meanwhile the almost decipherable murmurs, like conspirators', gave Peter an attack of the terrors more violent than he had ever imagined possible; his palsied body seeming to ooze as though it were running cheese, his mind half-paralysed with incoherent dread. Somehow the peril seemed to be far greater, the trap more ineluctable, because the voices were coming *up* to them from below.

However, after some incalculable interval, Peter made a brave effort. During a pause in the murmurs (it would, of course, have been far more prudent to have acted in concert with them – indication of his dismay), he edged even closer to the window, and tiptoed and craned his neck in order to gain an acuter angle of vision down past a jutting window-ledge. He could just make out a portion of close-cropped grey head, practically level with the gravel. Surely they couldn't be *crawling*? No, idiotic idea. It was simply that the pair of intruders were now sitting down on a charred wooden beam which lay against the entrance to one of the downstairs stalls.

Suddenly the grey head tossed back. A whinny ascended. J.D.?

The top half of Peter reeled back, from the waist, as though he had been struck. He saw Helen, who had one hand to her mouth, catching a soundless scream.

And this was the moment Lops chose to escape from his

house. He scampered into the room, executed an entrechat pirouette, and skedaddled back, and round and back again. He would betray them! Then he lay in a corner, all four legs stretched out, stomach heaving, nose twitching.

This absurd behaviour acted as a timely warning to Peter. Very well – so he *had* been unnerved by these unwanted visitors, following hard upon his dental catastrophe. But he must try at least to do better than Lops. He should return to normal breathing, and take time to consider where Helen could best hide (though in bedroom farces surely it was the lover, not the mistress, who was packed into the wardrobe?). But actually, now that he was calming down, was it not reasonable that Helen, anyway in a clothed state, should be in his house? So all they had to do was to dress very quietly, then sit with something to drink in their hands, waiting for a knock or bangs on the door. This was the obvious tactic he must recommend. Not being at all sure of the acoustics of his house, and certainly not wishing to add heavy treading to Lops's irresponsible scuffling, Peter made signs to Helen. He picked up a discarded sock, pulled it on while standing on one leg, then bent down farther again (still on one leg) to pick up a stocking of Helen's. Good! He hadn't tottered! Holding the stocking between little finger and palm, he pointed his index finger towards Helen's leg and padded with flat feet towards her. He leant to whisper in her ear – she had been following his movements openmouthed – 'We'll dress and drink. They might go away.'

Hardly the action of a conquering hero or masterful lover, but sensible enough in the circumstances.

# 15

Peter hadn't been able to fathom, as they sat waiting for the knock and the confrontation which never came, why Helen showed no signs of relief, but continued to be very taut and trapped-seeming by the idea of J.D.'s coming back. But he didn't press the point. It could, just possibly, be no more than shell-shock from their narrow escape, together with natural bashfulness at the prospect of meeting a former lover in company with a new one. Though somehow that didn't seem a complete explanation.

For the scrunches had faded down the drive, a car had revved, and it was a good two hours before Oliver reappeared alone – having returned to the hotel, enquired after his wife, and seen off J.D. on the small local train which connected with a Milan express. The three of them were now talking comfortably around the fireside. All perils surmounted, Peter felt immensely relaxed, satisfied, and amicably scornful of Oliver. Conversation meandered.

'Brought old J.D. round to see you,' said Oliver. 'Sorry to have missed you.'

'A pity we were out,' said Peter. 'Probably down in the gulley. Before the mist came up, was it?'

'Lots of scuffling noises upstairs,' said Oliver. Helen didn't blush.

'Lops, I imagine,' said Peter easily. 'You must meet him,

my tame rabbit. He escaped. Probably made the scuffling, I mean.' After all, he probably *had*.

'Hope you had a good time while we were slaving in Rome,' said Oliver. 'Enjoyed yourselves.' Peter decided these weren't innuendoes. Too heavy-handed, even for Oliver.

'Oh – J.D. said to tell you, darling, to let him know when you'd done the deed. Laughed. Some joke. Said you'd understand. Wouldn't tell me. I'm only your husband.' Helen looked uncomprehending, and said nothing.

Peter made a mental note to discover later, what this could possibly mean. He said, 'He was in good form, was he, J.D.? You were successful, I hope?'

'Oh – not really. It will all fall through, I expect. Only a sideline.'

Peter was not displeased to have this poor report of J.D.'s Italian undertaking.

'Poor Peter has broken a tooth,' said Helen. Peter looked gratefully at her.

'Nasty things, teeth abroad,' said Oliver.

'Yes,' said Peter.

'If they let you down,' said Oliver.

'Yes, though actually . . .' Peter ran a tongue over the jagged peak.

'Wouldn't fancy an Italian dentist,' said Oliver. Why did he harp on the subject? It didn't seem friendly. But Peter was in a forgiving mood.

'Oh, I don't know . . .' Peter looked at Helen. He would have liked to have been holding her hand.

'You don't *hear* much about Italian dentists,' said Oliver. That seemed to exhaust the subject. They sat in silence. How pleasant Peter was finding the recollection of adultery in tranquillity! Was it a dubious pleasure? Why? Peter enumerated the dangers he and Helen had surmounted as they scaled their way up the steep slope (surely now they were past the slippery bit). Falls, earthquakes, near-rapes, teeth, near-discoveries – Peter put them all in the plural, tied them up into a bundle, and threw them metaphorically into the flames. He even viewed a return, in the near future, to solitude with replete equanimity. The only thing to be done now was to settle his final account with J.D.

Really, he thought magnanimously, it might be enough simply to show Helen the compromising papers, and blacken him once and for all in her eyes. No need to pursue J.D. himself. Or was that shirking?

'By the way, we saw your girls at the station,' said Oliver.

'Not *my* girls,' said Peter. 'Did you talk to them?' he asked incuriously.

'J.D. thought your taste tophole,' said Oliver.

Well, Peter supposed that was 'fair'. Certainly he had in the past included them – singly, in pairs, even in triplicate – in his erotic fantasies, and even now could with little effort (rather as a greedy man, despite being satiated, is still able to indulge in balloon-thoughts of gastronomic delights) summon up delectable, if entirely hypothetical visions of their unexplored thighs. So Peter smiled, smugly unenvious that Oliver had fumbled those same thighs, and self-gratulatory that J.D. approved his taste.

Peter sought but failed to discover an acceptable way to phrase the thought . . . 'I am on top.' He looked towards Helen, who did not, however, reproduce his own contented and well-fed look at all. He could not tell what she was thinking and she seemed gentle and quiet and a little sad. Certainly not smug. Peter felt corrected – even rebuked – for his own self-satisfaction, which remained undiminished.

How everything had changed in the last few days! On his arrival, Oliver was the one who had patronized, seemed able to go where and do what he chose, was master of creation. Then Helen with her ability to understand and sympathize and endure, had seemed in the centre of things. And now it was his turn, he was calling the tune!

'Was J.D. looking well?' It was the first time Helen had

spoken for ages. She was poking a leg closer to the flames. 'He doesn't look after himself as he should.'

'You've always had a soft spot for J.D., haven't you?' said Oliver, rather nastily. A small red spot appeared over Helen's cheekbone, not so much a blush, more a sign of anger.

'Would you believe it, her thing with J.D. – darling J.D.? *Darling J.D.?*' he mimicked. 'Somehow can't bring myself to think of him as "darling". Though, of course . . .'

'I don't think we'll go over all that now,' said Helen.

'You've really got to watch this wife of mine,' said Oliver, the coarseness of his words scarcely veiled by a laugh. 'No, but you really must allow me to tell our friend Peter,' he went on. 'She's quite a girl . . .'

'Oh, shut up!' said Helen.

'The little jobs he gets you up to! Putting it like that makes him sound almost kinky, doesn't it? Old J.D. kinky! Probably past it!'

Helen sent Peter a look of apology. 'I'm sorry about my husband,' she said. 'He gets carried away.'

'Well, I'll tell if you won't,' said Oliver.

'As a matter of fact I told him all about it while you were away,' said Helen.

Peter naturally felt embarrassed by this sudden squabble, and put it down as part of the small-change to be paid for adultery. But he couldn't understand why Oliver should launch upon this tirade against an association which according to Helen, Oliver had himself encouraged. No doubt one could think of explanations why husbands should be especially resentful of affairs in which they colluded. But wouldn't that be attributing too much subtlety to Oliver?

Then Oliver did an extraordinary thing. He walked over to Helen, stood in front of her, and hit her. It was as violent and shocking as that. For ever afterwards, long after the dénouement of these events, Peter was to go over and over and over it again in slow motion, horrified, fascinated, unable to comprehend.

What actually happened, then, to reconstitute the action as far as possible, was this. Oliver was standing between Peter and the fire, clasping his hands behind his back like a soldier (or more precisely, a fat sergeant-major) standing at ease. When she had said, '. . . told him all about it while you were away,' he began to rock gently to and fro on the soles and heels of his feet, at the same time slapping the back of one hand with the palm of the other. Then without any change of expression, he walked or practically jogged over to his wife, six or seven paces away, springing slightly on his soles. He brought his hands from behind his back and squeezed them together in front of his chest in an attitude which in other circumstances might have looked devotional. For a second nothing happened. Then Oliver chucked Helen under the chin with one hand and lifted her head level with his waist, and with his other hand slowly and deliberately slapped her face. Not very hard but surely *too* hard, surely *much* too hard for it to be any sort of affectionate slap. Peter just sat, flabbergasted. Loath to believe his eyes, admit even the idea of such slow, cool boorishness enacted in front of him.

Oliver let go of Helen's head, ruffled her hair as if it had been a child's, and walked back to take up his stance before the fire, chuckling. 'It will all come out in the wash,' was all he said, before chuckling again, taking his pipe out of his pocket, and pressing the tobacco down into the bowl with his thumb, extra firmly.

During all this time, Helen had made no gesture or utterance of any kind. She was consciously contained, tense maybe, though it scarcely showed. Perhaps she was used to such disgraceful behaviour by Oliver, and had long since decided to treat it with neglect. Peter couldn't decipher what it was all about. Did Oliver suppose that Helen had told him about his request that she should, well, virtually prostitute herself in return for some deal with J.D.? But that didn't quite fit in. For one thing Helen had not agreed, and had become J.D.'s mistress only later. Indeed, Peter couldn't remember whether Oliver had ever been told about her eventual affair with J.D. – he had rather assumed not.

Oliver's brutal actions showed him in a new light. He obviously thought he could still subjugate Helen, at least in some ways. He wasn't quite so tame as Peter had supposed. Whereas perhaps he, Peter, was tamer – even although the failure to take sides in matrimonial warfare was, especially for someone in his position, very understandable.

It never occurred to him to doubt anything he had been told by Helen.

Still without uttering a word, Helen got up and walked her usual languid walk into the next room. There were scratchy noises and she returned, holding the palpitating Lops against her bosom. She stroked his ears and held him out for a second, so that the whole length of him wriggled towards her husband. 'He's a very comfortable rabbit,' she said. 'But I don't think he'll like the smell of your pipe.'

Peter was disappointed. He was hoping that Helen might say something to throw light on a few of the loose ends of their row, but, with Oliver puffing his pipe on the one hand and Helen cuddling the rabbit on the other, it seemed that they were in for a spell of silence. He would have to wait for an explanation. Now it was his duty to change the subject.

Affecting the appropriate stutter he said, 'Tomorrow I propose a picnic. After all, you've only got a few more days left now, I suppose. If it's at all fine.' Too late, he thought this might sound ungracious. No intimation had yet been made of their date of departure, but surely they could not be extending their holiday much longer. He felt the need for open air. Also, by the side of some mountain stream he could surely seize some chance to pick up the threads of his intimacy with Helen. And to resolve some of the ambiguities of the recent scene?

# 16

Liberation at every turn eluded Peter – his feet stumbling against some trivial obstacle, his eyes clouded by swirls of mist around objects which assumed new identities, or simply his teeth letting him down.

He regarded it as a considerable act of faith to have clutched at Helen as he had, and to believe that neither she nor his image of her would turn out to be subject to protean delusions.

But from the snares of what tyranny did he strive to free himself, anyway? He had not even defined any solid and reassuring enemy, unless you counted the forbidding statue of J.D. he had erected in his mind. While the real J.D., teasingly evanescent, seemed to decline physical manifestation nowadays.

Not, indeed, that it had been preferable in former years, when J.D.'s irruptions into his office, his sardonic contempt for Peter's bumbling 'idealism', had frayed and tattered his self-confidence. 'I should counsel you, my dear Peter, not to concern yourself unduly with intricate details of current policy. Yours is the role of the constitutional monarch. Not unduly onerous, I grant you. But you perform it charmingly.'

He had felt trapped then. Was he any the less trapped now? Yet, to go back again on his tracks, why ever should a feeble fugitive (such as he accused himself of being), an ambivalent and sentimental liberal, presume to imagine himself *chained* to the hillface with links which, after all, were of his own forging? Weren't words such as 'liberation' too grand for someone so sly and deceitful as himself? There, he had admitted it!

Peter was resolving these corkscrew self-accusations, as he lay awake and alone in the questioning small hours. He could not escape a few of the implications of his affair with Helen which was (he frankly acknowledged) born of irresponsible lust, loneliness, encroaching age and a dash of dislike for Oliver. Not a very attractive combination, certainly.

However, he would not dwell on that. He heaved himself over and lay on his other side. Nor (while he was lying on *this* side anyway) would he enquire into Helen's motives for surrendering her indolent sensuality to his after all not very importunate demands. Thoughts of Helen certainly formed a pleasanter avenue of thought, but the trouble was that J.D. seemed to obtrude there, too. While it was absurd to be jealous of her previous amours, she had perhaps not been altogether open with him over J.D. Out of tact, perhaps, a desire not to hurt him, nothing more natural. Still, that affair certainly reduced the significance of his own conquest. He instantly scolded himself for the use of the word 'conquest'. Women, he supposed, to their credit seldom used the word in such a connection. Oh, *socially*, yes – perhaps referring to their daughters, 'such a conquest, such a *nice* young man'. But in their self-communings? Then, he presumed, they thought more in terms of *giving* themselves, and that was the way he should try to think, too. But couldn't he attribute many of his failings and failures to just that – a lack of generosity? Too much scheming, too little giving?

Wasn't it shortage of generosity (it sounded like some electrical fault) that demeaned his spirit so? Or (and he promised to himself that this would be positively the last time he would turn over and lie on his 'tooth' side) to what extent did the hard little nub of his bitterness and resentment against J.D. act as a spigot which, once drawn out, might release a torrent of physical, spiritual and – come to that – even sexual energy?

A flood of light, far clearer than the dawn's, swept over him. He would make a full confession to Helen. He was sure he could contrive the opportunity. He would show her the incriminating documents against J.D. which he had stored, and burn them all in front of her eyes. It would be a genuine repentance. Reward would automatically flow, gush out. It would be an end to his cooped exile – of spirit, anyway.

So pleased was he by this resolve that he threw off the eiderdown, stood on the floor, and bit his fingernails trying to remember where he had secreted the documents.

It had been one of the first things he had done upon coming here. Surely he had knelt in that corner over there, and meticulously laid down on top of each other, rather as one might compose layers of tissue-paper to protect and pack some fragile possession, sheet after sheet of copies of documents 'borrowed' from J.D.'s secret files. He remembered the packing-up perfectly. He had been whistling or hissing through his teeth as he worked. And then what?

Ah, yes, he had topped up the hoard by piling in a few virgin sheets of paper, some unwanted paperbacks, and a very dog-eared dictionary. To fill the carton neatly to the brim, with the documents buried at the bottom, had seemed safer than to leave it half-full, possible prey of builders, liable to casual use as a wastepaper-bin in a forgetful moment.

The carton had been the identical twin of the one he had used to construct Lops's house. The fear flashed across his mind that he might indeed have used the same box by mistake. What a ridiculous loss that might entail of his damning evidence! Or rather, as he quickly corrected himself, of his opportunity for regenerate magnanimity! Peter sat on the edge of the bed again and buried his face in his hands. There were not many places in his house in which he could have hidden his cache. In the Tower Room on top of the new shelves? In the recess under the stairs, behind the kerosene containers? His limbs not yet fully woken up, he began to pad round the rooms, looking into probable and improbable corners; even examining Lops's house, turning up a corner of yellowed lettuce-leaf to see if there was by any ghastly chance a sheet covering the floor. Lops quivered in terror, but didn't scramble.

Peter was obstinate, and for at least half an hour continued his search upstairs and downstairs, without bothering to put on a dressing-gown or even slippers. He was determined to discover the documents before dressing, let alone before breakfasting.

He went on hands and knees to look under beds, stood on tiptoes to peer over a high ledge, and conceded defeat only after clumsily knocking down some pots and pans from a shelf on which – he had to acknowledge – there was not the smallest possibility of the carton's concealment. Picking up a saucepan, he turned it over, examined its interior myopically, and started to prepare his porridge.

Breakfast was the one meal over which he preserved English habits. It was not so much that he particularly liked the food, it was rather because he preferred a gradual awakening, one which veiled the lineaments of his new life. Indeed, after his interlude with Helen, to whose regime of coffee and toast he had gallantly yielded, he was relieved to revert to the familiar and complete meal – porridge, two eggs, toast, marmalade and coffee. However, inhaling the mingled steams of his cooking, he continued to fret over the whereabouts of his precious carton.

Of course, it would be possible just to tell Helen that he had destroyed the documents; but it would be far more edifying actually to burn them in front of her, after declining to allow more than the briefest, verificatory glimpse at their contents. Besides, truth at the moment seemed important.

Gawking at the grey sludge of his porridge he fell into despondency. Everything – the documents, the accusations in them, his new morning resolve, his own character, appeared equally grey. It was a passing minute. Once he bit into the toast and tasted the bitter marmalade he revived, even although a crumb of crust (which felt more like a boulder in the ragged valley of his tooth) reminded him of his urgent need to visit a dentist. This he could still fit in before their proposed expedition, if he stopped brooding and hurried.

The question was – which local dentist would hurt the least? Or be the most efficient, not necessarily the same thing? He imagined that J.D., or even Oliver and most of his other English acquaintances, would not hesitate to travel to Rome, possibly fly back to London, for such a major operation. Yet despite his usual timidity the thought of an Italian dentist did not terrify Peter; not even the possibility of a gleaming turret of Italian gold in his mouth perturbed him very much (he imagined he would come under pressure to choose gold as proper to his status as a 'wealthy' foreigner). He would consult his builders – why not? – who would be arriving within a few minutes. Peter did not consider such a source of advice to be eccentric. He had observed that both the labourers were men who looked carefully after their tools, their small motorcars and their families, and who dressed fastidiously on feast days.

Consultation took longer than he had expected. Sforza insisted upon his sitting on a chair, opening his mouth and allowing him to examine it. Peter's affliction encouraged an unwanted familiarity – '*che poverino! fa proprio male? Che guasto horrendo*', accompanied by appropriate mimings, hands held up against the cheek, eyes raised to heaven. One of their anxieties appeared to be that he might need to go without meat all that day; evidently they regarded him, as indeed he had regarded himself at the time of his mishap, as a confirmed carnivore.

Thrust against the back of his kitchen chair, his mouth opened to the sky, Peter felt himself in the classic position in which victims endure their tortures. Though his own subjugation was voluntary, he did not like rudely to hurry them. But at last he was allowed to get up. He blinked and shook his head to clear his mind, and placed the finger of one hand on the chair, rocking it on three of its rickety legs.

His examination had taken him beyond his normal threshold of embarrassment, so far beyond as to enable him to raise the other matter in his mind: the missing documents. Indeed, when he found it difficult to make Sforza understand the size and type of the carton, his reserve was by then so broken down that he was able to describe it as identical to that in which he kept his rabbit. The builders glanced at one another. A dictionary in one cardboard box, a rabbit in another! They were unable to help there. But they explained to him with even greater care and courtesy than if they had been addressing a sane man, precisely where the dentist lived – reassuring him that, although they were very pleased not to be visiting him themselves, he was an exceedingly kind man, unlikely to hurt him too much.

# 17

Even by the time Peter had confirmed at the hotel reception the address and reputation of the dentist, left a message for Oliver and Helen and parked his car, the morning still felt young. The brick-paved alleys looked as though they had been hosed and scrubbed, pots of geraniums outside doors and windows stood in order, there was still an occasional clatter of window-shutters being thrown open. The uncertainty whether he would get an immediate appointment formed the subject of a private bet with himself, and took his mind off possible torture. A slight shadow, but no more, crossed his mind as he realized he was passing the church looked after by his furious and false accuser; he crossed to the other side of the street and slunk quickly past, suffering from a mixture of vicarious shame for past indecency, and his own shame for present cowardice.

The cavernous silence that succeeded the ring of the bell, the dimness of the grey name-plate, and the door which swung itself open just as Peter was on the point of ringing a second or third time, gave him a sense of acting a part in some spider-and-fly scenario – as though he was being drawn by suction up the steep flights of stairs.

'You're my first Englishman,' said the dentist, ushering him in from the waiting-room and polishing his half-moon spectacles. The thought that, apart from white coat and shinier shoes, he bore a close resemblance to himself made

Peter feel queasy. He was exactly the same height, with the same stoop, the same thinning hair, the same short sight (which Peter trusted was no impediment in dentistry).

However, some of the surroundings at least seemed propitious. The long beaks of the familiar instruments, shining as brightly as the dentist's spectacle-rings, looked efficient enough. A polished, eighteenth-century walnut tallboy, with pigeonholes cram-full (he imagined of maps of mouths) struck a pleasantly incongruous, domestic note. Only an ashtray with some half-a-dozen viciously-stubbed stubs, and a circular litter-bin covered with (of all things) a transfer of English huntsmen in full cry, seemed shabby, unsuccessful, improvised. Also there was no welcoming young female attendant, although a rustling and scuffling of papers next door possibly indicated her presence.

Once the preliminaries were over, and Peter was shrugging his shoulders to 'feel' his back against the chair and adjusting his head upon the head-rest, he recalled Oliver's comment that 'somehow one doesn't hear much about Italian dentists' and reflected that one of the reassuring reasons might be that dentists everywhere were more or less the same, practising their universal craft; a set of teeth (like a set of sins for a priest) was both absolutely individual, and yet incredibly similar all over the world; needed and developed the same sort of firm expertise – the international language of the drill and the injection.

It was while he was starting to discuss suitable treatment, not yet encumbered by mirrors, gags and probes in his mouth, that he caught sight of an English dictionary on one corner of the window-ledge. Surely he recognized it! On the other hand, there was no reason on earth why that copy should not resemble his own? It was no odder, indeed less odd, than that he should resemble the dentist. Both were standard editions. Both were in an equal state of dilapidation. Again there is no reason why dictionaries should not be tattered and dog-eared, rather the reverse. But didn't the position of the ink-blot under the 'C' of the title exactly correspond with that on his copy?

'You're learning English,' Peter said, casually rinsing out his mouth with the reassuringly familiar pink water.

'Not me, my assistant.'

Peter tried to think, as he lay back ready for fresh probes (and who has ever exchanged more than one question-and-answer at a time with a dentist?) when he had last seen his own old English dictionary. Then it dawned on him. He had placed it on top of *those* papers, in *that* carton, for which he had been searching only three hours or so ago. He looked round as much of the rest of the room as his angle of vision would allow him – past the frieze of huntsmen, in and out of the legs of the instruments, in the wild suspicion he might see his lost box lurking in the corner.

Once more made to lie open-mouthed and stare at the plaster-casts of Victorian *putti* on the ceiling, he heard a door open and close behind his chair. With more gallantry, and less consideration for his patient than his English equivalent would have shown, the dentist halted his examination, laid down his tool, spread out his arms, opened the palms of his hands upwards, brought them together to his mouth, and blew a kiss. This destroyed Peter's wishful thinking about the universality of dentists. Peter now cricked his neck to glance over his shoulder, and from the corner of his eye caught sight of long dark hair, a drawn-in waist and a nurse's starched white overall. He failed to adjust his vision until she – whoever 'she' was – was standing on one side of the room, with her back to him, silently mixing a tiny potion. He approved the way she tossed her head, presumably to clear her hair from her eyes, and didn't blame the dentist for his blown, if still unprofessional, kiss.

It wasn't, however, surprising that Peter didn't recognize her until she turned round. One does not expect to see people one knows in dentists' surgeries – apart from other patients in their waiting rooms. Peter could imagine Oliver saying that, coarse snob that he was. Still, he agreed with him. Anyway, as she turned round and walked towards his chair, swaying slightly and blinking under the weight of her long black eyelashes, Peter recognized her from his captive viewpoint level with her breasts, as one of 'his' girls (all three of whom he had up till now thought of only as students). Was she, he wondered as she bore down on him, now going to place her foot on the chair's pedal and raise him upwards until they slowly came almost face to face?

However, exclamations followed. Peter stood up and for a few seconds they formed a curious social knot under those *putti* on the ceiling, gesticulating and chatting away – the dentist and his assistant doing much the most of it – as though over cocktails. That would never happen in England. As soon as decorum was restored, and Peter duly elevated and tilted, his thoughts started to ramble. He was intrigued, pleased to be thus further diverted from dental preoccupations. An injection was made. His rambling was of a very vague kind, for the prospect of imminent physical pain, he found, deconcentrated his mind wonderfully. Was this where his box had indeed come to rest and were all his papers still in it? (*'Rinse please'* – a fizzier rinse than was usual surely.) Had they been read, had they been kept or destroyed? They had been in a rinse-pink office file, simply marked 'J.D.' How had he been so inconceivably careless? There had been a few letters of his own in the box, too. Rather embarrassing love letters. Very old ones, though (*'rinse please'* – and the girl placed another big flat pill at the bottom of the mug, and filled it up). Could the letters have been the subject of all that giggling with Oliver on the night of the small earthquake and imagined rape? No, surely not? If he didn't get all his papers back, might he still retrieve just one or two sheets, as a token? Ah, numbness! His mouth belonged to the dentist, was in another world and he was happy to let it go. But trust? If he raised his new-found love for Helen into the realm of trust, might this not be an occasion for them to forge a bond of mutual faith in each other? For her to accept, without evidence, that she had so cured him of bile, so softened his poor heart, that for her sake he was truly willing (and willing was all he could be, if the papers had really vanished) – to destroy all remnants of his hope of revenge?

Peter looked at the girl's long dark hair, imagining it could fall very sleekly and disorderly over shoulders that were probably cream-coloured (ivory? cream? how could he best unclothe them?). In the light of his odd angle of vision, probable pain and diminished consciousness, his imaginary infidelity was very minor, and easy for himself to pardon.

He made a mental list of things to ask her as soon as he was back on his feet. Her part in the fiesta, her progress in English, the health of her 'missing' friend whom he had not seen since the earthquake, her opinion of Oliver (too difficult that, perhaps) above all the whereabouts of the documents.

He himself had little to offer: an invitation to his house, a promise to cheer the fiesta floats, the English plural of 'tooth', the final and outright gift of a tattered dictionary.

He caught sight of the stupid round face of a large, cheap electric clock. He had been only twenty minutes in the chair. Soon, in the outside world where powder puffs of clouds floated in a dim un-Italian sky, Helen, Oliver and he would be sitting by the side of a stream, unwrapping the salami.

At the end of his minor ordeal, 'The dictionary is useful, I'm glad to see,' said Peter, rushing in headlong, forgetting all the gallant compliments ('if I were Paris, I know to whom I would give the apple'). 'Oh, and there were some papers, I seem to remember. They're not here, by any chance?' Peter stood a little awkwardly, sweeping the air with one of his hands to find a suitable resting-place for it. He could not decide how long it was permissible to stay chatting in a surgery; for the girl had now twice disappeared and returned in response to bells and buzzes.

Now she came close up against him – did her eyelashes really brush his cheek? – and stroked the lapel of his coat with her manicured fingers, in a way which would have been caressingly familiar if only it weren't so impersonal.

'I'm slow and stupid,' she said. 'Not clever like you.'

'The books, though, did any of them amuse you?'

'We told your large friend. Has he returned from Rome?' Her answers weren't answers at all. Peter couldn't stay for much longer.

'There are a few things I'd like to have back, if possible. They were in the box. Do you remember seeing a pink folder, lots of letters and papers in it, and so forth?'

'But I was just going to tell you,' said the girl, as the dentist left the room. And she opened both her eyes and her mouth very wide, like a doll. 'Didn't your friend tell you? We gave them to him and he put them all in his car. We thought we were doing you a good turn, that's what your friend told us. Weren't we?'

'I don't understand. I mean, *what* did he tell you?'

'Just that the letters were important, he'd take them back to you, they'd be safe with him.'

'The subject came up . . . ?'

Peter began to feel awkward at the length of their conversation, its interference with the dentist's profession.

'He's very fond of you. We talked a lot after that earthquake. Then later on – oh, he called to patch things up – some misunderstanding, he'd never behaved *badly* – and we showed him the books you'd given us. He seemed to think them funny, why? He's got a very loud laugh, hasn't he?'

# 18

'So they may well be in your car now.'

'You really are extraordinarily careless,' said Helen affectionately.

'I suppose I could look for them now. It seems a pity to interrupt "us" though, while Oliver is doing his "little explore". What an odd expression it is – that "little explore". Odd because Oliver is so large. Big men shouldn't say doing a "little" this or that.'

'Childish habits? Sign of insecurity? I suppose I'm so used to it I don't notice any longer. Anyway, "little explore" is just what he does. He goes up on a mound and walks round and round it, putting his hand to his brow. We should take a photograph of him.'

'He doesn't mind looking fat? Taken from beneath?'

They were sitting by the side of the stream which Peter had scouted out days and days before. It was still too early in the year to dabble their feet in the mountain water, though the sun was agreeably fierce. The neck of a bottle of wine, breasting the current, could be seen wedged among some white rocks. Altogether, at least on the surface, it was an idyllic scene, almost exactly as Peter had dreamt. Only the cloud of the Missing Documents shadowed their happiness.

'It seems silly in a way,' Peter said. 'Making such a fuss about finding them. I mean, looking for something you're going to destroy anyway. How shall I do it, by the way?'

'You could burn them one by one. It would take longer than you think. How many papers are there?'

'Well, the file's this thick. Paper boats would take too long, too.'

'Only a man would think of paper boats. I expect you played with them as a boy.'

'Thousands of words floating down into the Adriatic. Rushing at first, then getting drowned, or soaked in those stagnant green estuaries. Rather a suitable end for J.D.'s sordid intrigues.'

'Peter, just give them to me.' There was a fair silence. Helen lay on her back. She didn't touch Peter or hold his hand as she spoke. Peter said, 'I'm not really a destructive person, that's the trouble. Would you say? If you divide humans into destroyers and destroyed, I'd be one of the latter, really.'

'Too gloomy a way of thinking for now.' Indeed, for two people, one of whom was half in love, sitting under the sun by an Apennine stream, the tindery smell of maquis in their nostrils, perhaps it was. A sense of transience might be an excuse. A buzzard hovered, head lowered, before swerving at a tangent to the crest of a foothill.

'More buzzards than clouds in the sky now,' said Helen.

'All right,' said Peter. 'But I'm not a creator, I'm afraid. I used to think I could create a philosophy – no, that's too grand – but at least a way, a mood of life. Vaguely beneficent to all. But I haven't even created a proper marriage, or a family. It's soppy – do schoolgirls still use that word? – but I have created a spark of love for you. Even if it was born idly out of lust, it's a tiny hope.'

'What are you going to do now?, asked Helen. 'Once we've gone away for good? I hate leaving you. Will you be all right?'

'I expect so. I've always been able to manage on my own

in most ways, except for some knots which I can't untie by myself. You've untied the worst one.'

'You make it too easy for me,' said Helen mysteriously. 'But I can't explain now. Look, there's Oliver come back.'

And yes, Oliver had been working his way round to the far bank of the stream, and was now standing opposite them, deciding not to get his shoes wet. He didn't look like a paddler. The reflections of the ripples on his face and hat made his expression shimmer and wobble, broke him into a jigsaw.

'He can't hear us,' said Peter. 'That's practically a waterfall – a very small waterfall, as you'd say.'

Helen waved to Oliver, picked up an apple and threw it into the air, a gesture indicating that it was time to eat. Oliver turned and started to clamber up a steep path leading to the bridge.

'And how would Oliver destroy the papers?' went on Peter. 'I can't see him using paper boats. Just tearing them up and stuffing them into little bins? Panting rather angrily as he did it? Perhaps he *has* destroyed them. Is he a destroyer, do you consider?'

Half of Oliver – hat, head and shoulders – could be seen some way above them, starting his march across the bridge.

'I've told you before,' Helen murmured, 'Oliver doesn't count, though I don't like saying it.'

'I don't like hearing it, really, either,' said Peter.

During the picnic Peter again and again attempted to pursue the subject of the papers, while Oliver shunned it with bland inconsequences. Sinister, Peter thought, he's lost them. Helen, too, seemed to have lost interest.

'You didn't say anything about them to J.D. when you were in Rome, I suppose?' he asked Oliver, peeling a banana.

'There's that buzzard again! Or is it a buzzard? Might be a peregrine. Lost my glasses. Any idea of the size of beastie those fellows can gobble up? Mice all right. Rabbits too big.'

'The girl at the dentist seems to have liked you. She said she saw you just before you left for Rome and gave you the papers to bring back to me.'

'Shouldn't leave papers lying around dentists. Bound to lead to trouble. I say, isn't that a fish?'

'They weren't really important. Except to me. No state secrets.'

'Well, we'll have a jolly good dekko after lunch. Expect they're still hiding themselves under the back seat. Thought they were a load of old bumph to tell you the truth. I say, look at Helen sunning herself.'

It irked Peter that Helen remained so silent. After all, it was due to her redeeming influence that he was making all this fuss. However, by now the papers (so long, indeed, as they were lost) had become symbolic; and symbolism, he told himself, means less to a woman.

To search a lightly-loaded family car, even one as untidy as Oliver's might be presumed to be a gentle post-prandial exercise, which would fluster nobody. Oliver and Peter set about it in carefree collaboration, Peter rather relieved to be doing something, and to be spared Oliver's banalities and evasions.

Wrenching up the back seat, and coming across the accumulation of tops of ice-cream cartons, worn out Biros, give-away toys of cereal manufacturers and old chocolate wrappers gave Peter brief nostalgia for England and confectionery.

But then there came the snag. Oliver could not open and examine the boot because he had lost the key. To be more exact, he must have lost his bunch of keys including the ignition key (he confessed with embarrassment) inside the boot. He must somehow have left them inside while extracting the picnic hamper. He tapped on the roof of the car as though tapping his teeth. This brought no inspiration.

Then he banged on the roof, and kicked one of the tyres. Then he used all his weight to bear down on the boot, so that it bounced rather suddenly. 'Poor show, poor show,' he repeated. It was not clear whether he was disparaging himself or the car.

They were marooned. Excusably if illogically, Oliver continued to cast some blame upon Peter. 'Must say your blessed documents have done a first class job of burying themselves.' But as much as he would doubtless have liked to call off the search, he had no choice but to continue his perspiring efforts.

For her part, Helen was unperturbed – and possibly pleased – by the contretemps which allowed her more time to bask in the spring sunshine, careless of the discomfiture of her husband; and not particularly caring for Peter's either.

Oliver had now found a screw-driver, and had half-disappeared head first into the back of his car, groping and rooting as though in a rugger scrum. He appeared to spreadeagle himself over the top of the back seat. Evidently he was trying to detach it as a means of rear entry into the boot. 'Dismantle the whole bloody thing,' he muttered crossly.

As he contorted his head still further towards the rear window, he reminded Peter of some burrowing animal, a giant mole perhaps. Too cumbersome a prey for the buzzard, certainly. Constipated grunts indicated progress and frustration in turn, the former also producing a fairly calm exhalation of breath, the latter a tetchy snort. Disdainfully and unhelpfully – but what was there for him to do? – Peter imagined the working of the tendons of Olivers' thighs as he wrenched and unscrewed and wrenched. How clumsy Oliver was! Peter found it obscene, disgusting, it reminded him of Oliver's relation to Helen, he shut his eyes into the sun until he could see yellow and fire-red nebulae. That made him dizzy, but upon reopening his eyes he was able to develop, as he leant against a convenient outcrop of grey rock, an emotional blank, a fatalistic indifference to the outcome of the search, or to the dissolution of the car, or to their protracted stay in the wilderness. At least, Peter selfishly thought, he was 'whole' now. His tongue told him of the regular formation of his teeth, he had no need to limp, he was at peace with Helen and not even in any real conflict with the struggling monster Oliver.

At last the back seat, hoicked out, temporarily littered the riverbank, giving it the appearance of the down-at-heel environs of a country garage. Oliver was sweating and triumphant. The bunch of keys was quickly retrieved. A plaid rug lay in a dark of the boot, and Peter was reminded of Helen saying that she felt like a 'chameleon on a tartan rug'. Finally, amongst the débris, a glimpse of pink showed itself. Peter was now assisting in the search, but wasn't quite quick enough to beat Oliver's pounce, who held the file aloft like a bullying schoolboy and said with a 'funny' foreign accent. 'Not so fast, my friend.'

One sheet of paper slithered from the file and floated zigzag towards the ground. 'Please look out,' Peter said feebly. 'Please don't start a paper-chase.' He spoke as quietly as he could to conceal his agitation. 'My price,' said Oliver, still with a trace of his stupid foreign accent, 'is that you should reveal the mystery of the Pink File. What's in it, old chap?' he continued, using his normal tone of voice.

'Give it to me,' said Helen, pleasantly, without getting up from the ground. 'Neither of you can be trusted with it.' 'There's nothing mysterious, really,' said Peter, feeling – or perhaps creating – tension. 'Just papers of mine I want for the record.' 'All about J.D., eh?' Oliver said. 'Wouldn't do for J.D. to see them, you mean?'

Helen got up, lightly and affectionately touched Peter on the arm, and walked over to take the file from Oliver's hand, which had come down in surrender. 'You're like children,' she said. 'Both of you.' Then she moved away a little, and stood with her back to the stream and the men. After a few seconds she turned round. 'Anyway, it's empty,' she said. 'Just blank sheets.' Her face was white.

# 19

Peter detested Rome airport. In this he cannot have been alone. Gusts, alternately too hot and too cold, blew from ventilators in all directions; lost groups scurried in all directions, bewildered, bedraggled and dwarfed; scraps of announcing voices clanged from overhead, from underneath. All airports – but Rome is the supreme example – are halls of dispossessed tribes, whence they are ejected centrifugally to destinations that are unlikely to welcome them: will, indeed, eject them in turn. Individual courtesy and cleanliness, which so mitigates the ordinary run of Italian anarchy, has deserted these metallic regions. Not even in the biblical Babel can people have lost so much dignity and purpose as the solitary bedouin (of all people the last, one would have thought, to lose dignity) whom Peter saw fidgeting, and kicking a torn newspaper with one toe of his highly-polished shoes – probably bought that afternoon in the Eternal City.

Peter had come to bid farewell to Helen and Oliver. Perhaps Oliver was the one human being whom Rome airport did suit; his aimless bustle and his artificial bonhomie being perfectly in tune with his surroundings.

They were trying to order whiskies at a long counter. Oliver said, 'Funny! Old J.D. Just seven days ago. Put out the red carpet for him all right. Oh to be a VIP!'

Someone jostled Peter and kicked his leg away from its

perch on the bar-stool. Oliver continued to speak, waving a large spotted handkerchief at the distant barman.

'Oh yes, oh yes. You should have seen him arrive. Old J.D. certainly knows how to get attention all right. Some high-up wearing an outfit like a grey frock-coat. All smiles. Three bags full. Quite a different cup of tea. Straight into a Rolls-Royce, too. A Rolls-Royce!'

'Pity it all came to nothing,' said Peter mildly.

'What! My dear fellow, J.D. pulled it off! Quite a coup, really.'

'But I thought you said – I'm sure I remember – that it didn't come off.'

Oliver chortled away. 'Did I? Must have thought that's what you'd like to hear, I suppose. Oh, no, quite the contrary. Great success.' Helen laughed.

'You're getting quite Italian, darling,' she said to Oliver in a tone which struck Peter, to his surprise, as quite affectionate.

'Cunning old bastard. Things often seem to "come off" with J.D., blast him. Didn't relax, of course. No holiday. Not till we stopped off to see you. Different chap by then – weight off his shoulders.'

They collected their whiskies at last. They were hemmed helplessly in and clutched their glasses close to their chests.

'Glad to hear it. In a way, I suppose,' Peter brought himself to say.

'You mustn't imagine I don't know what you think about J.D.,' went on Oliver. 'Known all along,' Oliver said this in an unpleasant tone. Or perhaps it was the whine of an incoming plane. It was impossible to tell.

'I've been cured, really,' Peter said to himself more than to Oliver. 'Purged of my feelings towards J.D. now.'

'Don't imagine J.D. cares tuppence about your feelings for him!' said Oliver. 'If that's any comfort to you. It was something J.D. said – Oops,' he finished, slurping some whisky down the narrow interstice which separated their two bodies.

'You know I keep on thinking about those missing papers. Do you think by any chance J.D. did see them? He travelled quite a bit in your car, didn't he?'

'Not all the time in the Rolls!' echoed Helen.

'Perfectly possible,' said Oliver. 'Perfectly possible. After all, how was I to know? Now you bring it up again, J.D. did say something.'

'But that's important,' said Helen. 'Try to remember.'

'Well, I'll search the old memory-box if you give me time. And if you can hear me above all this rumpus. You know J.D. uses that confounded silence of his? So when he does laugh it can be pretty unnerving? Not that he generally laughs at anything I'd call comic. "Crool" really.' He dug Peter in the ribs.

'You do him an injustice,' said Helen. But Peter thought this showed more percipience on Oliver's part than he generally gave him credit for.

'Well, you don't often sidetrack old J.D.' Oliver rambled on. 'I'm speaking of excursions now, trips, that sort of thing. J.D. likes to go from A to B. In a straight line. Can't think why he got it into his head to visit some old monastery at the far end of a godforsaken valley. Well, we drew up. Cold at that height. J.D. got out of the car. "If I'd been an abbot," he started – '

'Just like J.D. to say "abbot" rather than mere "monk",' Helen interrupted.

' – "Which God might understandably have forbidden," J.D. went on. "I wonder what penance I'd have devised for poor Peter." I took your side, old man, and asked why he thought you'd be a candidate for penances. "He doesn't even have the courage of his crimes," said J.D. Bit hard, that.'

'Poor Peter,' said Helen.

Peter wasn't sure whether he was hearing correctly. His

ears seemed to have taken over as his chief distorting organ – the whining zooms and clatter around him seeming to become properties of Oliver's narrative. Was it the monastery he had himself failed to reach? Peter asked, attempting a jocular tone of voice, 'I told you about my own unsuccessful walk to a monastery, didn't I? Those oxen, that long ridge, all the mist?'

'Of course, that's the one! All comes back. Told the story to J.D. myself on the way up. Passed the time as we drove. Certainly amused him. "How like him to fail," that's what he said, I remember. Rather unkind. Not sure he didn't decide to visit it just so as to be one up on you. Suppose you could be flattered, in a funny sort of way. Not far off our way, of course. *Very small* detour.'

Peter was reminded of Helen's saying '*very small* earthquake'. There was no possible connection – no – but the brevity of the detour added to his ignominy, the echo of the phrase to his disquiet.

'Anyway, J.D. said,' Oliver went on, ' "The punishment he has chosen for himself would not be a wholly inappropriate one for an unsuccessful blackmailer. Solitary confinement in one of the less comfortable cells. With an occasional visit from you, my dear Oliver, as an extra titbit." After J.D. said this, he began laughing, like I told you. "It is of an incompetence past all crediting. Even for our incompetent friend. Though not without its humorous aspects." Something like that. And then J.D. went on laughing fit to split the old sides. Thought it odd at the time. Couldn't see what was so funny. Not sure I do now.'

Peter said, 'You think he'd seen the papers? Is that what you mean? Read – even took them? They were pretty well *incriminating*, you know . . . ?'

'Do we need to bother now?' said Helen. 'I'm feeling terribly tired. All this standing, and noise.'

'So now we admit it!' crowed Oliver, wagging the little finger of the hand he held his whisky glass in. 'Naughty!

Shouldn't have tried to blackmail old J.D. Should have known better than that!'

But Peter said nothing. He was pretending to himself that he had not been going to blackmail J.D. Not really, ever. He was telling himself that he had never laid actual plans for using the papers. They were just a sort of reserve power. And, anyway, since his confession to Helen he had become a different man, had untied his spiritual knot. So why couldn't he enjoy the irony of having given up something which had already been taken from him? Why should he grudge *that* trifling defeat – if defeat it was – at all?

Try as he might, though, it irked him that his grand renunciation should be made to look so foolish. He hoped that Helen would be charitable and recognize that he had nevertheless earned his liberation. Indeed, without her recognition what was it worth?

Oliver was bellowing on. 'Never likes showing his hand, old J.D. Knew better than to tell me what it was all about. Stood out a mile, though, that he thought you were planning to get up to monkey tricks.'

Peter couldn't bear Oliver's jovial hostility any longer. He felt as though an attack of asthma or migraine was about to come on. Or possibly of both – he was suffocating and his head was aching. Oliver had now lit a cigar and in the curling tendrils of its smoke Peter fancied he saw Oliver's gross thoughts ascending as a djinn. He was convinced that Oliver knew that J.D. had found and taken all his papers even although he couldn't recollect anything very precise that Oliver had said. If, indeed, Oliver ever said anything precise.

Peter could forgive Helen for her failure to come to his defence. The circumstances, anyway, made it impossible for her to transmit any consoling reassurance. But could she see from his eyes how hounded he felt?

'I hope our plane isn't delayed much longer and I don't want another drink. I'm bored with this conversation,' said

Helen. Though expressed ungraciously, Peter was thankful for this faint signal of commiseration – for such he took it to be.

To his astonishment he now noticed that Oliver was turning green. There was no doubt about it. He checked the colour by the bartender, by the row of bottles upside down on their optics. None of them matched Oliver's green. It was the green of boiled spinach – stale, over-boiled spinach. Peter didn't think that comparison unfair. He watched with fascination as Oliver let his cigar fall to the ground and the colour of his face darkened. Helen was observing, too. She said, not unsympathetically, 'You're being punished for something. You're turning green.' Oliver replied stiffly, drawing himself up, 'Green isn't the right colour.' 'That's what I said,' repeated Helen. 'It doesn't look right at all.' 'I've never heard such a tomfool idea,' said Oliver in a high, unsteady voice. 'One isn't punished by turning green.' 'Perhaps talking of J.D. has made you feel unwell,' said Helen. '*You* don't mind doing his dirty work, do you?' said Oliver – and barged through them, marching erect with remarkable self-control, an Englishman attempting to preserve his dignity, on a forced exit to a foreign lavatory.

## 20

Peter was later to reflect that had it not been for Oliver's indisposition and the plane's outrageous delay, he would probably have been left forever in blissful ignorance – at least about Helen's part in the affair.

So perhaps it was a mistake to have interrogated her. Put it down to the disintegrating effect of the airport, axing the mind, splintering it into fragments.

Helen and he had secured Oliver a bench on which he could lie at full length, heaving and panting. He now looked more like a whale than any of the previous incarnations of his visit – pig, mole, etcetera. Afterwards they had strolled, for want of anything better to do, through the jungle of one of the car parks, the monster inhabitants of which glistened and shimmered like waves in the refracting sunlight. They did not hold hands, not because it was too hot and sticky, but rather because they felt the estranging curse of their surroundings.

Back in the Babel, after a quick look at Oliver, they sat down to share a bench with a child who was buffeting her toy, possibly out of affection, possibly just to restore it to shape. It was a large white rabbit, which naturally reminded Peter of Lops, and of the last time they had seen him. Something had been said then that came back into his mind – yes, it was Oliver saying that J.D. had wanted to hear from Helen 'when the deed was done'. Something like that.

Peter crossed his legs, twiddled his thumbs, and embarked upon the course of questioning that was to destroy him: 'Oliver is always so sarcastic about you and J.D., isn't he? I can't stand it. I feel I want to get up and defend you. Almost physically. Why is it?'

'It doesn't matter – can't you see?'

'But it does, to me. Really, I admire the way you put up with him. I hate to think of your leaving now, and going back with him.'

'It doesn't matter,' repeated Helen. It seemed all she could say. But instead of quieting Peter, it drove him on.

'Jealousy, do you think that's it? Is that what you meant about green being a punishment? Is Oliver really so very jealous still of you and J.D.? Absurd, considering all you told me. And so long ago. It's me, I suppose, he should be jealous of – a bit, anyway, I hope.'

'We should really go and see him soon. We shouldn't leave him lying there, like death.'

'He keeps on referring to the dirty work you do – or did for J.D. I don't understand that. What was it, anyway?' So as to disguise the importance of his enquiry, Peter bent down, picked up the rabbit (which had fallen to the floor) and dusted it down.

'You won't forgive me. Or perhaps you will. There's no point in going into it. That's a very large rabbit, Peter. It doesn't suit you.'

But all Peter did was to worry at Helen's reference to forgiveness, tweaking the rabbit's ear.

He said, 'But why ever do you suppose I have anything to forgive you for? I mean, to me . . . ?'

'It's much too late to make confessions. Too hot, too crowded, too absolutely pointless.'

'But don't you see, I hate letting you go without *knowing* – even if I do run the risk of irritating you.'

'You're not exactly *irritating* me,' said Helen (and, of

course, as soon as she said this Peter realized that he *must* be; it's not a phrase people use otherwise).

'Please go *on*,' said Peter, with a faint sinking qualm – the feeling of a loser.

'I don't *want* to – I don't want to be beastly – you might remember that afterwards, Peter. You seem to be asking to be told the truth. Braver of you than usual.'

'You say it almost as though you despise me, a little,' said Peter ruefully.

'Isn't there always a tiny bit of that in . . . what we've done? No, Peter, I'll always be fond, grateful: it's myself I should despise if anyone.'

Peter began to grow extremely uncomfortable. He returned the rabbit to the little girl. That gave him a breathing space.

Helen went on, 'It's not that I've been a Mata Hari for J.D.; not exactly. I'm not the Mata Hari type, wouldn't you agree? But it's – well – you must have asked yourself how it all happened so quickly (I won't say easily)?'

'Well, we understood each other,' said Peter, lamely.

'Let me explain a little more to you about J.D., to see if you'll still forgive me. He isn't a blackmailer like you, Peter, don't think that. But there was a time when he only had to lift a little finger and I'd do anything he told me. If I'm to be absolutely honest I daresay I still would. Do you understand? Don't suppose it's because I'm still in love with him, I'm not. I don't understand why it is, but I need to do what he says. More than *you'd* do anything *I* asked, say. Much more, I'm afraid.'

Peter was sick and tired – literally – of the spectre of J.D., with which he had been shadow-fighting for so long. He realized, half in panic and half with relief, that it was probably now too late to avert Helen's revelation, the nature of which he was beginning to guess. Panic gained the upper hand. He sought desperately to stall. For the first time in his life, he hoped that Oliver would appear, loom over them, accidentally spring the trap he was caught in.

He was unable to look at Helen, for fear that he would be forced to see her with new eyes. The unangelic voices of the announcers added to his hunted instinct to scurry (if he possibly could) and hide somewhere.

Was it too late to run for refuge, back into the sanctuary of ignorance? *Anything* was better than that he should cease to cherish Helen in his fancy. He said, 'Don't tell me. There's no need. I'm never going to desert you – never in memory at least.'

But it was too late for Helen to stop. 'All *my* fault,' Peter thought, clenching his hands. '*I* started it, *I* asked for it, I can't blame *her*.'

She insisted gently, 'It's better that it should all come out. Perhaps it's selfish of me; but if it's any compensation, it's because I'm so fond of you that I want to give you the choice of forgiving me or not, once you know everything. I'll be very, very brief. Actually, all I need say is that J.D. knew all along that you had those famous papers, and asked me – instructed me – to get hold of them, wheedle them out of you, anything, but on no account to return empty-handed. Do things fall into place now?'

All Peter allowed himself immediately to register was that this confession desolated him, totally. He snicked off all further awareness or thought. He determined to petrify his being by an act of will. If he froze, if he stayed absolutely still, if he did and said absolutely nothing, it would give him a few seconds – or an eternity, it was the same thing – to absorb the shock. After the 'eternity' he allowed himself a partial recovery of consciousness, and some strictly inconsequential actions, like saying 'Lops' under his breath, and gazing at a scrumpled-up scrap of tissue on the next-door table.

As for tying up loose ends, or things falling into place, or whatever it was that Helen had said, there could be a lifetime for that.

Here was a wound over which he could run his tongue for ever, a bunch of keys to a masochist's paradise. He wondered whether he could manage to say anything, he felt himself quivering, and decided to utter in order to test his nerves. But he couldn't think of anything to say. So he stammered, listening to himself to hear if he squeaked, 'Please, I don't think I can say anything. Nothing about forgiveness, nothing like that. I'm dumbfounded, you see, I think that's the word. But don't . . .' his voice trailed off. Searching for 'the word', or rather letting it come into one of the few channels of his mind which he permitted to remain open, gave him momentary relief. Or not 'relief', exactly – more 'extra time' during which his feelings could be left untouched, in suspension. Ah, self-torture by a thousand qualifications!

Almost inconceivably, so much so that he wanted to shriek (he was being torn up by the roots) Helen went slowly on, closing her confession by offering him a very vinegary sop: 'And yes, I think, I think – and perhaps it's the worst thing but I must say it – that Oliver may have known all along. From some of the awful things he's been saying. I'm not absolutely sure – but I've been casting my mind back.'

'I didn't imagine you were in collusion,' Peter managed to say.

'That *would* have been inconceivable.'

## 21

Towards the end of the return journey, back by rail to the city nearest his farmhouse, Peter had had plenty of time to go over and over the events of the previous few weeks. Seeking to banish the revengeful fantasia which sleeplessness can induce, he continued diligently and fondly to exculpate Helen. From some of the things she had said on parting – 'I've grown so fond of you, that's why I must tell you everything' – he extracted as much comfort as he could. It was pretty lukewarm. He tried not to let words like 'treachery' form in his mind, he continued to deploy his enfeebled brain to delay the shock, he refused to think of the conversation which, even now, Helen might be having with J.D.

Only when he thought of Oliver did he bare his teeth in a grimace of revenge – forgetful of his fellow-passengers, who edged nervously away, or glanced down. Some young soldiers stared insolently at him, amazed.

How to explain that after-earthquake incident with the girls?

'Given you something to *read*, has he, the old devil?' – that fragment of Oliver's conversation, wafted over the café table after his fall, came back to him. Perhaps Oliver in the theatre hadn't been attempting to seduce the girls at all (indeed, fumbling was clearly all it *had* amounted to) – but had just been jollying them along, had seized the chance when everyone was upset, to get them to tell him everything they knew about Peter. 'Spill the beans,' as Oliver would have put it. Oliver wasn't nearly such a fool as he liked to let himself appear – Peter was bound to recognize *that*.

And Helen's agitation on the morning after the earthquake? That was harder to explain. Could Oliver perhaps have said something about 'papers' to Helen over breakfast that morning – just enough to lead Helen to suspect that J.D. *might* have employed Oliver as well as herself on the mission? 'Divide and rule' – very like J.D. And not very amusing for Helen.

Next, why had Oliver slapped Helen in that extraordinary manner, after her and Peter's near discovery together? Well, suppose J.D. had told Oliver in Rome, or on the drive back after Oliver's delivery of the papers, that he'd put Helen up to getting the papers back, too. So that Oliver would have known about Helen's game, but not *vice versa*. (Oliver, of course, had lied to him all along.)

Whichever way he looked at it, and so far this meant that he was just able to acquit Helen of any collusion with Oliver, he had certainly been duped more than Helen had allowed him to believe – or perhaps known herself. Peter's head jogged up and down with the movement of the train, like a puppet's.

They now laboured up a long valley strewn with boulders, amongst which lay a few scattered and splintered pine trees abandoned by foresters, as not worth the hauling. Blobs of rain briefly wobbled on the window, before slanting away backwards. Peter shivered. He caught himself peopling the landscape with hostile homunculi. He really must stop. If he began to do this in the relative comfort and company of a crowded carriage, it would be a poor lookout for him when he returned to his solitude, to the whine of the chimney of his kerosene stove in the night winds.

The train rested at the small halt on the top of the pass.

There seemed to be a great deal of clucking and flurry of poultry on the platform. Two passengers bundled somehow into Peter's carriage, bringing with them fresh air and animation. One of them wedged herself between the soldiers almost directly opposite Peter. Her face seemed vaguely familiar. She stared at Peter with malevolence and with such fixity that Peter was constrained to lower his eyes, past the wisps of grey hair on her chin, down to the magazine on his lap. Then timidly he swivelled his head sideways and half-upwards to look again out of the window, at the disused water-tower standing at the end of the long platform; and the train moved slowly forward.

He searched his memory. Surely this was the aunt, the fearsome old lady who had brayed at him from the flat above the chapel! He succumbed to a desire not to let her go scot-free for all that unjustified railing. To punish her a little would divert him from his brooding.

'How well your niece is looking – I saw her again last week,' he said jerkily. Even as he spoke he felt a ridiculous temptation to apologize instead of attack. He lowered his eyes still further and saw a hen under her seat. It had been very quiet. The sight relieved his tension and he felt happy to remain silent, too. At last the old woman said, 'Your friend the Englishman came to see us several times. Everything was explained. It was the earthquake. Everything was upset. His wife came, too.'

This half-apology surprised Peter. It struck him as being un-Italian, the wrong way round. A beaming smile, effusive insincerity would have been normal, surely. However, her expression remained unfriendly. Perhaps this reflected anger at her loss of face. Or perhaps it might be that she simply didn't like him?

Then a jerk of the train recalled him to what she had said. So Helen had accompanied Oliver to the flat! But she had told him nothing of this. Of course, there could be an easy explanation. Helen might have had a row with Oliver about his stupidity, his long absence after the earthquake. And Oliver could have pleaded innocence, and arranged a confrontation to prove it. There would have been time for all this, certainly. But the fact remained that Helen had not told him. And an abyss seemed to open up beneath him as the train gathered speed and curved tooting down to the cities of the Adriatic.

But, curious thing, Peter could not in his heart feel sorry for himself. Partly because he was able to discipline himself not to do so; but more due to the reflection that he had deserved his misfortune, even to his being betrayed. This was not exactly stoic of him. Glimmers of conscience – scarcely more than self-awareness, not strong enough to have prevented commission of adultery or the contemplation of blackmail, not strong enough now to pervade him with remorse, nevertheless sufficed for him to blame himself. And the scorn he felt for himself, though faint, was real.

Peter looked with admiration at the grim face of the old woman opposite him. It was so fixed, so uncompromising. He did not intend to battle with her. But he could not resist asking, 'She came often, did she, my friend's wife? They've just returned to England.'

'Twice perhaps. Three times, I don't remember.'

They were now winding underneath those steep slopes on which Peter had lost his way, in his attempt to walk to the monastery. He remembered the shepherd who had said, 'poverty makes slaves of us all'. He wondered whether it was not truer to say that cheating makes slaves.

And whether courage, *almost* regardless of its aims, was not the most admirable of the virtues. Peter was, of course, too intelligent not to qualify the thought.

At the junction Peter resolutely took a separate compartment from the old lady and her hen, and completed the last stages of his brooding journey home. This train was merrier, small and nimble; it stopped and started suddenly, and didn't fit in with Peter's mood at all, on account of which he felt unreasonably irritated.

Lops at any rate would be at home to welcome him, he thought in an access of sentimentality which provided a consoling layer between 'himself' and the extreme depths of his depression. He had been absent for only three days and had left, he remembered, adequate lettuce and clear instructions to the builders. Even if they could not fathom his attitude ('*eat* it, surely he must *eat* it soon'), they would respect his wishes. And Peter had no fear that Lops would escape; he knew from experience that he would not stray far into the wilderness.

Peter felt as if he himself was an insignificant animal, trapped in a noisy moving cage, carried to a destination that was little more than a prison.

Towards dusk he squelched back into his home, cursing the sodden clay which stared up yellow at him, shielding his head with a newspaper from the ferocious, near-sleet which streaked in on him from the mountains now barely visible in the middle distance.

Once inside, he went straight to where he had left Lops's lovingly-decorated house. The carton was empty. He upturned the few faded lettuce leaves on the floor. Then he cooed and searched everywhere. There was no sign of him. Braving the rain, he searched outside, too, among the rafters. There was nothing for it but to wait till next morning and cross-examine the builders.

Peter spent a very bleak evening. The thought that Lops at least would not desert him had been an absurdly effective anodyne.

Towards nine o'clock, after a cold supper, he went for a final prowl. The moon had risen and the rain had stopped. To his delight he saw a small creature sitting on the length of hosepipe which – left outside – slithered like a snake all along the length of the house.

However, the creature proved not to be Lops. It stayed

motionless as Peter approached. He could clearly make out a very round head, two small peaked ears and a grey, furry body.

He stooped to peer at it. Still it didn't move. It was a baby owl! Peter bent down farther to pick it up. He felt no twinge of disloyalty in the discovery of a new pet – why should he? It felt warm and soft in his hand, and trembled without attempting to spread its wings and fly.

There was a screech. A shadow flew between Peter and the moon. He sensed, rather than saw or heard, the swoop and whirr of great wings. Instantly, his head was struck by hard talons. It was so lightning that (letting drop the baby owl) he had no time to cry out with fright. No pain came, and the baby owl was ferried away to safety on a long, low flight, by its courageous mother.

A warm trickle ran down Peter's cheek. He put his hand to the blood. Only then the agony started.

Much later, nursing his poor wounded eyesocket, he was to spare a thought for Lops, and wonder whether he had met a similar fate – at the claw, perhaps, of an even more fearsome bird of prey.

In any case, a new chapter of torments had begun for Peter. This time, he did not think he had deserved it.